Perfec

EMMA CARTER

Heartline
Books

Published by Heartline Books Limited in 2001

Copyright © Emma Carter 2001

Emma Carter has asserted her rights under the copyright, Designs and Patents Act, 1988 to be identified as the author of this work.

This is a work of fiction. Names and characters are the product of the author's imagination and any resemblance to any actual persons, living or dead, is purely coincidental.

All rights reserved. No part of this publication may be reproduced, stored in or introduced into a retrieval system or transmitted by any form, or by any means (electronic, mechanical, photocopying, recording or otherwise) without the prior written permission of the publisher. Any person who takes any unauthorised action in relation to this publication may be liable to criminal prosecution and civil claims for damages.

Heartline Books Limited and Heartline Books logo are trademarks of the publisher.

First published in the United Kingdom in 2001 by Heartline Books Limited.

Heartline Books Limited
PO Box 22598, London W8 7GB

Heartline Books Ltd. Reg No: 03986653

ISBN 1-903867-24-X

Styled by Oxford Designers & Illustrators

Printed and bound in Great Britain by
Cox & Wyman, Reading, Berkshire

EMMA CARTER

Emma Carter is a shameless romantic. A doctor, she fell in love with her husband Pete one moonless night when they were on safari in the middle of Africa. They lay for hours holding hands and gazing up at the Milky Way, which felt close enough to touch.

Ten years on, the couple live in a wooden tree-top house surrounded by bush and close to beaches, but the bedroom has a glass ceiling so that every night when they walk upstairs to bed, they can look up and see the stars without having to camp any more. Life's not all romance though: the windows leak when it rains, possums scratch at the door and tumble across their roof every night, while sulphur-crested cockatoos sometimes try to eat the house – but it is a wonderful setting for an author.

Emma says: 'My favourite sort of hero is strong and powerful and very sure of himself, yet at the same time warm, loving and very human. I find men like that extraordinarily sexy. I hope you do too.'

chapter one

Dr Tessa Webster was alone in her room in the Maternity Unit of Wellington's Karori Hospital for Women and Children when Nathan looked in. She was hunched over her bed with her arms spread apart and her head squashed into the mattress but she looked up the instant the door squeaked. 'Nathan,' she gasped. 'Thank God. I was about to buzz for you. The baby's coming.'

'Yep. So I hear.' Despite the flushed bareness of her face, the ragged mop of damp, dark curls cascading around her shoulders and the shapelessness of a hospital nightie that would have made almost any other pregnant women resemble a pumpkin, his colleague still looked, he marvelled, utterly gorgeous.

He didn't understand how Simon could have walked out on that.

Privately he might consider Tessa vastly better off without her ex-partner but still it appalled him that other man wasn't even in New Zealand for this. Knowing Simon, the father of Tessa's baby was probably blithely unconcerned, downing cocktails and flirting with bar girls in some tropical resort.

But now he thought about it that was probably just as well, Nathan reflected contemptuously. Because if Simon turned up now, then after seeing Tessa struggling without him for four months and now going through labour on her own, he'd be tempted to heave him out the window.

'I've been speaking to your midwife.' He came in and took her hand when the tightening of her face and the change in her breathing told him her next contraction was beginning. 'She says you've had five hours of contractions and you're doing great.'

When her contraction eased, he reached behind her to the stack of pillows on the bed. 'Your back will feel the strain less if you have more support. Lift your arm.'

'I don't want pillows.' She twisted her head away from him, pushed her head against the bedding again, and made a tight sound in her throat. 'I need you to help me give birth.'

'Always in a hurry,' he teased. 'Warp speed ahead, as usual, even in labour.' He saw the savage look the comment earned him and hid a grin. The hospital functioned as a medical referral centre for complicated pregnancies and Tessa's job, like his own, often involved caring for mothers and babies through difficult births. Given that history, it wasn't surprising that Tessa had grown anxious now it was her own turn.

'Hey, take your time,' he soothed, changing his tone. 'Relax. Trust me. Everything's going beautifully. The baby will come along when he or she is good and ready and trying to rush things isn't going to make one bit of difference.'

To distract her he retrieved the cream and red bouquet he'd bought from the florist in the hospital's foyer. 'Where will I put these?' he asked, looking around. 'By the window in a vase or will that be too sunny for them?'

'Nowhere. I hate Christmas lilies. The smell makes me sick. Get them out of here. Nathan, I'm serious. Listen to me, please.' She lowered her head again for another contraction. 'The baby,' she gasped, 'is…coming. Help me onto the bed. Stop mucking around, there isn't time.'

'Focus on your breathing.' He opened the door and

threw the flowers onto a chair in the corridor and came back to Tessa, frowning. Irritability was common in women during the transition stage of labour but Tessa couldn't be anywhere near that yet. This was her first pregnancy. By every rule in the book she had to have hours to go. 'You're working yourself up prematurely.'

'You don't understand…'

'I understand that everything's going according to plan. Try some gas. It might take the edge off the pain enough to help you feel calmer.' He reached across the bed and connected the tubing to the mask and offered it to her. 'OK, OK,' he discarded the mask when she bared her teeth at him, 'you don't want that.'

As the registrar on duty for the weekend he had overall responsibility for supervising all mothers and deliveries but he hadn't planned on examining Tessa because she'd been admitted under the private care of the department's senior specialist. When the other man had checked her on arrival he'd reported that although he was willing to agree to Tessa's demands to labour naturally, he expected it to be prolonged venture. 'Something stronger then,' he suggested.

She reached around to the bedside trolley, grabbed a packet of sterile gloves from the equipment tray, and threw them at him. 'Put them on. Now.'

Nathan let the packet fall onto the bed. 'Pethidine?'

'I don't want an injection.' She sounded furious. 'It's far too late for that. I want you to deliver my baby. Nathan, pleas…' She broke off momentarily. 'Listen to me,' she continued, gasping. 'I have to push.'

'Tessa, sweetheart…'

'Don't patronise me!' Her face contorted. 'I might have

done two years less obstetrics than you but it's enough to know when I'm having a baby and I'm damn well having one now. I can't stop pushing.' She broke off and her face clenched again. 'Don't stand there staring at me, you monster. Help me!'

'Pant,' he ordered. 'Keep panting. Whatever you do, don't push. You cannot be ready for that yet.' He made for the door. 'I'll call the boss.'

'No!' Tessa lifted her head and he saw she looked desperate. 'Nathan, don't leave me. Don't you dare leave me. If you walk out now I'll hate you for the rest of my life. I don't want him. Mr Austin's been trying to talk me into a Caesarean for the last month. I don't trust him. He thinks my pelvis is too small, but I know it's not. The baby's small enough to be fine. Then he said the baby wouldn't rotate but it did. He said I'd be in labour for days but I can feel it moving the right way already. I know I can do this. I don't want him. I want you. Don't leave me, please.'

Nathan was already back by her side. He massaged her narrow shoulders through the damp cotton of her gown, trying to ease some of the tension he could feel trembling through her. 'Shhh. OK, OK, I'm staying. It's all right. But try to relax.'

He kept up the massage until her stiffening beneath him warned him her next contraction was coming fast. He knew touch now would only irritate her and he released her and buzzed for the midwife who'd been leaving to grab a meal when he'd arrived He retrieved the gloves she'd thrown him. He tore open the paper covering then left them on the trolley, eyeing her consideringly. 'I need to check now.'

'I know. That's what I've been telling you. Get on with

it,' she gasped, bracing herself hard against the bed again for a few moments until he saw the contraction ease. 'Stop wasting time,' she moaned, grabbing onto his arm to help herself up onto the bed. 'I don't have any modesty left after this performance.'

But he didn't have to check internally. He saw as soon as she was on the bed how far on she was. 'The baby's crowning,' he accused.

Her face creased strongly and she groaned. 'I told you!' She twisted her head from side to side, her expression agonised. 'You should have listened to me.'

Nathan's attention focused on her baby now, he supported the infant's head with one hand as it rotated, freeing up a sterile suction tube from the stack on the trolley with his other hand so it would be there if there were problems after the speed of the delivery and he needed it. 'Slowly, Tess,' he urged. 'Puff. You're doing great. Take it easy now. Keep puffing.'

The door swung open and Claire Davies, Tessa's midwife, beamed at them both. 'I've finished tea,' she announced cheerfully. 'How are you going, Tessa? Nate, if you're hungry there's plenty of macaroni cheese...' But she broke off and Nathan, who had no more time to look at her, felt her astonishment.'

'Open the delivery pack,' Nathan ordered. 'We'll need a shot of Syntometrine in about thirty seconds,' he added, referring to a mixture of two drugs they used to encourage strong contractions. 'Good girl, Tess. Push now. That's it.'

The statuesque midwife scrambled to prepare the injection and then to tear open the packs containing swabs and guards and the clamps he'd need. 'Should I call Mr Austin?' she asked urgently, pouring antiseptic from a sterile bag directly into one of the dishes in the delivery pack.

'No time,' Nathan responded.

'No!' Tessa spoke at the same time as him but her answer came out as a roar. 'I don't want that butcher anywhere near me. Claire, keep him away. I want Nathan. Nathan…?'

'It's all right,' he soothed. 'You're doing fine. Blow now. In and out. Good, Tessa. You're doing well. That's perfect. OK, as soon as you feel it I want one more big push.'

She delivered the baby's little head into his hands and he supported it while the first then second shoulder emerged and then the rest of the infant's body followed in a controlled rush.

'Congratulations.' He smiled. 'You have a little boy.' He wrapped the infant in the towel and lifted him up, reassuring himself that the baby's colour and breathing and movements were normal before passing him across into Tessa's trembling, urgently outstretched arms.

'A boy,' she whispered, her blue eyes huge. 'Oh!'

The infant's little hands clutched at her fingers and he stared up at her and she stroked his face wondrously. 'A boy.'

Nathan clamped and cut the baby's cord then returned to the other end of the bed to wait for the placenta to emerge while Claire helped unbutton Tessa's gown and guide the baby to her breast.

'I can't believe it,' Tessa murmured, glancing up at him later once he was able to come back to her side. Her smile was beatific. 'I can't believe how beautiful he is.'

'He is beautiful.' Looking down at the tiny baby cradled in Tessa's arms, Nathan felt a surge of tenderness. Lightly, he stroked the infant's soft, downy cheek. 'Hello, Tiger.'

'Thomas.' Tessa touched his cheek. 'Thomas Mitchell Morrison. Thomas was my father's name and Mitchell was both Simon's grandfather's and my grandmother's name,' she added when Nathan looked at her questioningly. 'And Morrison after Simon of course.'

Nathan, busy adjusting the blanket Claire had arranged around the baby to keep him warm, didn't believe Simon's short-lived contribution to Tessa's baby warranted recognition, let alone Simon's surname, but he kept that thought to himself.

He's going to be stubborn like you,' he warned instead. 'Look at him.' He smiled as the baby's tiny fist bashed against her gown when his mother shifted a little. 'He's inherited your determined little chin.'

Tessa smiled. 'No, he's going to be placid like his father,' she murmured confidently. 'Aren't you, my love?' she asked her son. 'You're going to be placid and easy-going, like your daddy.'

Simon? Nathan looked at her. If deserting your pregnant lover was classed as placid, easy-going behaviour, then he prayed Thomas would overcome his genes and grow into a fierce and fiery man. 'Tessa, I'm sorry to take him away from you but we need to examine him.'

'I know.' Tessa passed the baby to him. 'Of course.' She smiled again. 'I'm sorry I was rude to you before. And I feel terrible about being so awful about your flowers.' Her eyes drifted to the door. 'I hope someone's looking after them. I don't know what came over me. I love Christmas lilies usually. They're such a special part of this time of the year. I'm so sorry.'

'I'll live.' He unwrapped Thomas into the warmth of the open, pre-heated incubator Claire had set up. 'The flowers might not but you had a lot on your mind.'

Claire weighed and measured Thomas and administered his vitamin K and clipped identity bracelets around one wrist and ankle while Nathan examined him.

'I'll give him a quick wash when you've finished,' the midwife announced. 'Tessa, what about you?' Claire went back to Tessa and rolled her to one side and then back as she quickly changed the bed's linen and then Tessa's crumpled gown. 'A nice sponge bath or would you like a pot of tea first?'

'Tea,' Tessa answered promptly, and Nathan smiled as she settled herself back into her freshly-made bed with something of the air of a satisfied cat. 'Thanks, Claire. I am dying of thirst.'

A squawk from Thomas earned Nathan a sharp glare. 'Nathan, you brute, are you torturing my baby?'

'He didn't like having his mouth opened.' Part of his routine examination of babies immediately after delivery involved passing his little finger into their mouths to check for palate deformities but Thomas hadn't appreciated his efforts. Keeping the baby wrapped to preserve his warmth – newborns had some ability to regulate body temperature but they were still vulnerable to cold stress – he lifted Thomas up, cradled him in his arm, and smiled down at him. 'He wants his mummy.'

'Of course he does.' Tessa held out her arms for him. 'All right?'

Nathan nodded. Despite his early arrival Thomas seemed a healthy, sturdy infant. 'What about you?'

'Oh, fine.' Flicking a sheaf of dark curls back behind her shoulder, she gazed down at her son and rocked him. 'Sore and tired and revoltingly sweaty of course, but fine. And very, very happy.'

He smiled. 'So exactly how did you manage to do that so fast? You know it's not supposed to be easy the first time.'

'Lucky I guess.' The two dimples at the sides of her mouth deepened as she beamed at him. 'I knew I had to push. And that'll teach you for being so patronising. If you'd ignored me one more time I'd have ripped your head off. You're the one who's always saying that mothers know best but suddenly when it comes to me you assume I'm clueless.'

Nathan had returned to the shelf by the incubator where he was writing up the required notes on the delivery and Thomas but he looked up with a lazy grin. 'I should have known better.'

'Yes you should.' Her smile was warm enough to melt metal. 'But thanks anyway,' she added. 'Sorry again about being so horrible to you. I'm very glad you were here. I always wanted you to do the delivery. I only went to Mr Austin because he would have been offended if I didn't and I didn't want to wreck my career prospects.'

Nathan felt incredibly flattered. 'It was a privilege to be here,' he told her sincerely. He finished his notes then went to the bed and bent and kissed her cheek warmly. 'Congratulations again. I have to go. I'm due in Theatre at six.'

He'd admitted a twenty-five-year-old woman with severe abdominal pain. Ultrasound hadn't been helpful in sorting out the cause and since the surgical registrar who'd looked at her didn't believe the pain was appendicitis, he needed to look inside her pelvis.

'I'll look in later,' he promised Tessa on his way out.

Obstetrics and Gynaecology at Karori took up one side of the double-winged complex, while the Paediatric

Department occupied the other. The main operating theatres were on the top floor and the junior doctor on duty with him, Honour Te Rapua, was scrubbing in Theatre Two when he walked in. 'Hey, Nathan!' she called. 'The nurses told me Tessa was admitted in labour this afternoon. How's she going?'

'Thomas Mitchell Morrison, two point seven kilos,' he revealed. 'Mother and baby both doing fine.'

Their scrub nurse lifted her brows. 'No Caesarean? I heard Mr Austin saying earlier that he was sure she was going to need one.'

'Normal delivery,' he corrected. 'After a fast labour.' Privately he wondered how long Tessa had been having contractions at home. Far longer than she'd admitted, he suspected. She wouldn't have been keen to come into hospital early. 'Five hours.'

Honour, busy helping Nathan swab their patient's belly, said, 'Do you think Simon will come back now?'

'You're kidding aren't you?' Ngaire, the senior scrub nurse, rolled expressive eyes above her mask. 'What Simon Morrison should do and what Simon Morrison actually does are never the same,' she announced briskly. 'The man's a selfish pig. If poor Tessa's hoping he'll jump on a plane and come rushing back from his great journey of self-discovery because she's given birth to his son, she's in for a big disappointment. I have never, never understood what she sees in him.'

Nathan looked up in time to catch Honour's startled look. 'He's very good looking,' the other doctor offered.

'Too pretty,' Ngaire argued. 'He's the sort who spends hours preening in front of mirrors at the gym. You can never trust a man like that. He's never appealed to me. No, I've got my eyes on Nathan here.' The nurse flashed her eyes up at him. 'I've been waiting two years for you to corner me in the instrument room, Nathan. When's it going to happen?'

Nathan met her flirtatious look mildly, then lowered his eyes to the patient's abdomen. 'Ask me again if Donald ever comes to his senses and boots you out,' he told Ngaire teasingly. The nurse was married to one of Wellington's most senior surgeons and the couple had a set of school-age twins and a new baby girl. 'Scalpel.'

'Scalpel.' Ngaire put the handle of the instrument into his palm. 'All kidding aside, you're Simon's friend, Nathan. Why do you think he ran off?'

'Acquaintance these days more than friend,' Nathan said tightly a few moments later as he inserted his second probe.

'But you introduced him to Tessa.'

'Years ago.' He wasn't proud of the fact. He and Simon had been at boarding school together, but while Nathan had gone on to university in Dunedin in New Zealand's far south, Simon had opted for a science degree in Auckland. Restless after a year, the other man had switched to law for a term, then to commerce, then back to science to finally complete his degree. But he'd still been dissatisfied and after taking off a couple of years to work as a ski instructor and tour guide, he'd applied for medicine.

The delay meant that although he and Simon were the same age, both two years older than Tessa, Simon had been a long way behind both of them in his medical training. When Simon, bored with Dunedin, had transferred to Wellington to finish his studies, Nathan had done his best to help him settle in. Tessa had been working with him at the time and he'd introduced them.

The idea that Tessa might be attracted to Simon had

never occurred to him. Tessa had only recently come though a broken engagement and she'd still seemed upset about the break up and the last thing Nathan had thought that anyone feeling vulnerable and hurt would have needed would be someone as egocentric or intransigent as Simon.

Not that Simon was entirely to blame for his nature, Nathan admitted. His friend's upbringing had been unsettled and insecure and he'd never felt as if he belonged anywhere. He'd spent most school holidays with Nathan's family at the farm. While Simon had never lacked cash – his father had had a top model BMW convertible delivered to school the day after Simon earned his driving license – he'd lacked parental supervision and attention. The adult Simon could be a gregarious, generous and easy companion but he was also restless and self-absorbed and easily bored.

But as it became obvious that Tessa was happy with Simon and that she loved him and clearly felt she could depend on him, Nathan had been forced to acknowledge that he'd underestimated how much Simon had to offer her.

The couple had been together for three years when news of Tessa's pregnancy first spread through the hospital. Nathan, like most of their friends, had offered his congratulations, but instead of the celebrations everyone expected, Simon had disappeared.

A week later Tessa revealed that Simon had decided he wanted to see more of the world and that he'd resigned from his Casualty job and flown overseas. Nathan didn't know how long he was planning to be away or whether he intended returning at all. Tessa was a close colleague and a very good friend and he couldn't not have noticed the occasional moments when she seemed to be struggling to maintain her usual effervescent, chatter-box personality, and he worried about her. But she was as independent as she was stubborn and she didn't accept help readily. Even when it had been obvious to him that she was virtually dropping with exhaustion at work on long shifts late in her pregnancy, he'd sometimes had to physically propel her out of the hospital before she'd give in and accept his insistence that he was going to cover her duties.

'But what do you think, Nathan?' Ngaire gazed up at him. 'Will Simon pull up his socks and jump on the next plane and fly back to help her?'

'I think that it's none of my business.' Nathan made his first incision.

He wrote up his notes after the operation, caught up on what was happening on the wards, then checked on Tessa. But both Tessa and Thomas were asleep. 'She's worn out, poor mite,' the nurse in charge of the ward murmured, coming up beside him. 'She had a shower and a sandwich then nodded straight off.'

'Nathan?'

They'd started walking away, but Tessa's voice calling to him brought him around. She was standing in the doorway to her room and he realised they must have woken her. 'I'm sorry...'

'It's all right.' She looked pale and sleepy but she interrupted before he could finish. 'I was trying to stay awake to see you. Do you have a few minutes?'

'Of course.' He came back to the room and went with her inside. 'Did the boss visit?'

'He was disappointed he didn't get to cut me open.' She

grimaced, then went directly across to the bassinet and looked down at her sleeping baby. 'I need to ask you a huge favour.' She gazed up at him now, her shadowed blue eyes seeming huge in her pale face. 'Will you ring Simon for me?' Nathan drew back but she spoke before he could answer. 'I'd do it myself except I don't want him to take it the wrong way.'

Simon? He made an effort to conceal his disgust, reminding himself for the umpteenth time that he had no business interfering. 'You know where he is then?'

'I've had a postcard,' she said hesitantly. 'He's in Thailand, at a resort on an island. He says it's the most beautiful place in the world. He's doing a dive course and he's planning to base himself there for a few months. I looked up the website and found the telephone number. If *I* call him he'll think I'm trying to pressure him into coming back. If he wants to come back of his own accord then that will be wonderful but I don't want him to feel forced.'

Nathan could think of a few pleasurable ways he wouldn't mind forcing Simon at that moment. His so-called friend needed to be reminded that life couldn't always be a careless, irresponsible jaunt through paradise. 'What do you want me to say?'

'That he's a father.' She looked down. 'If he seems interested you could give him the details.'

If he seems interested? 'He'll want to speak to you.'

'No he won't.' Her small smile just about broke his heart. 'That's the last thing he'll want.' She retrieved a sheet of paper from the top of her bedside table and a bundle of coins. 'This should be enough.'

Nathan waved the coins away. 'I'll call from my office,' he told her. 'They'll bill me eventually. Are you sure about this?'

'It's right that he knows.'

'I could use my mobile and call from here.'

She shook her head. 'I don't want to hear. And please could you tell him that I hope he had a happy Christmas and that I hope he got my card.'

Christmas was three weeks back. He'd been on duty that day and Tessa had come into the hospital and joined the celebrations at the hospital. The thought that Simon hadn't even bothered to call her appalled him. But he nodded.

'Thanks.'

She sounded calm and totally controlled but as he opened the door into the corridor he glanced back briefly and saw her folding her arms over her face.

chapter two

The call wasn't straightforward. The number Tessa had given him turned out to be a Bangkok booking office for the resort rather than the hotel itself but eventually he was given the correct number and finally he was put through to what a gentle voice assured him would be Simon's bungalow.

When it was answered in German by a sleepy-sounding woman he thought there'd been another mistake, but it seemed not. 'Simon,' she repeated. 'Oh, just a minute please,' she added, switching to flawless, barely-accented, English. 'He is taking a shower to wash off the sand from swimming. Hold the line please.'

When Simon spoke a few moments later, Nathan said coldly, 'Tessa wanted you to know she's had the baby. A boy. Two point seven kilos. She's called him Thomas Mitchell and she's giving him your surname. Congratulations.'

'A boy?' Simon swore. He sounded dazed. 'Wow. I guess that makes it all real now,' he went on raggedly. 'That's early isn't it, Nate? I wasn't expecting – a month premature or something, is it?'

'Fifteen days.' Nathan's fist curled hard around the receiver. He could hear the voice of the woman who'd answered the phone in the background and Simon made a muffled reply. He waited a few moments before interrupting, 'I expect you're wondering about Tessa.'

There was nothing for a few seconds then Simon said in a sheepish voice, 'Oh, Tessa. Yeah, of course.

Em...how is she?'

Wanting you, he wanted to say. Needing you. But he confined himself to a gruff, 'She'll live. She hopes you had a good Christmas. She sent you a card apparently.'

There was another space then Simon went on a bit stiffly himself now, 'They don't do Christmas here, it's Buddhist. I'll get someone from the hotel to order flowers for her. I'll ask for roses, Tessa's always liked roses. Does the sprog look like me then?'

'Not in the slightest,' he revealed coldly. *Flowers*? That was the extent of Simon's acknowledgement of the birth of his child? If the other man had been in the same room as him he recognised he might have throttled him then. He wasn't aggressive by nature and it disturbed him that his reaction to Simon lately suggested he still possessed, even at a latent level, impulses that verged on the violent.

In the background he could hear talking again and a few moments later Simon said in a stilted voice, 'Nate, we're in a bit of a rush. We're going around the other side of the island for dinner and the boat's due to leave any minute. Becoming a father's a good excuse for a few bottles of beer and a big cigar tonight. Give Tess my love. Thanks for the call.'

He hung up before Nathan could answer.

Tessa was sitting upright in bed holding Thomas when he returned to the ward. She looked up eagerly and Nathan's heart sank. 'Did you get him?' she asked breathlessly.

He said carefully, 'He's going out to have a cigar and whisky to celebrate. He said to give you his love.'

'Oh. That's nice.' She looked unsure. 'He didn't say anything about perhaps coming home for a little while to see Thomas?'

'Thomas being early seemed to come as a bit of a shock. He didn't sound as if he was ready for it. He won't have had time to consider his plans yet.'

'No. I suppose not.'

But the way her dark lashes fluttered down to conceal her eyes was like a dart of pain straight into his chest. 'I'm sorry,' he offered awkwardly, his regret sincere even if he wasn't sure of the best way to express it to avoid embarrassing her. 'About Thomas. About things not working out the way you might have planned.' He thought about the German woman sharing Simon's room and wanted to hit something. 'You know that if there's ever anything I can do…'

'I know. Thanks.' She didn't look at him. 'You've been very kind.'

'He's not worth it.'

'Yes. So everyone keeps saying.' But she still wouldn't look at him and her careful smile wasn't remotely reassuring because he could see behind that to her pallor and the stiff, rigid way she was holding herself. 'Thanks again for everything. You must have loads of things to do. Sorry I've taken up so much of your time today.'

Nathan would always have all the time in the world for Tessa, but it was obvious he wasn't wanted now so he lent across the bed and kissed her goodnight. 'Try and get some sleep. Doctor's orders. You too, little man,' he added softly, stroking Thomas' dark hair when the baby stirred.

Tessa stared for a while at the door after Nathan left. It hadn't been fair of her to ask him to talk to Simon, she knew. He and Simon had been friends long before either of them had known her and Nathan had to have divided loyalties. But she hadn't known whom else she could trust. Nathan, alone of all the people she knew, had never railed against Simon for the way he'd left her.

But that was the last time she'd ask him for anything, she vowed. She'd let him do far too much for her already. She'd kept a tally of all the extra hours he'd worked for her covering her shifts towards the end of her pregnancy, and she intending paying all those back, but there'd been so many other favours she'd probably never be able to return. He'd spent hours helping with her garden. He'd cooked meals for her when she'd been so tired after work that all she'd wanted to do was lie down and put her feet up. And his help with converting Simon's old study into a nursery for Thomas had made the task a weekend job instead of one that would have lasted months if she'd had to tackle it alone. Plus she'd never forget his kindness in coming with her to her scan appointments so she had someone with her who could share her joy at the sight of her baby.

He worried about her, she could see that. But from tonight she would be so strong and so independent that he wouldn't feel any need to be concerned any more.

Strong and independent and happy.

In her public moments at least.

She knew it might take her a little time before she could be that way all the time when she was alone. She was scared about how it was going to be raising Thomas on her own. She worried about whether she was going to be a good enough mother to give her son the perfect upbringing he deserved. But she was determined to be strong and positive because she had no choice about that. Someone was depending on her now and she'd do everything within her power to fulfil his every need.

Her gaze lowered to her son and her heart gently warmed and filled with love. Such a tiny person, she marvelled. Such a tiny, incredible, perfect little person.

She'd been allocated a single side room on the ward, meaning she didn't have to feel bad about disturbing anyone else's sleep when she had to ring for a nurse in the early hours of the morning to help her position Thomas for his feed.

'I know I should be able to do this,' she admitted apologetically, embarrassed at the difficulties she was having and Thomas' obvious frustration at her lack of success. She'd expected breastfeeding to be something they both took to naturally but instead she found herself feeling awkward and clumsy. 'I know all the theory.'

'Which means nothing when it's your own baby.' The nurse sat on the edge of the bed and smiled. 'You have to find what works best for both of you. Try holding him in the fold of your elbow like that,' she suggested, adjusting the pillow under Tessa's arm then moving Thomas to fit. 'Just so both his head and shoulders are square onto you. Now let his cheek brush you to trigger him to open his mouth more like a yawn. Good.' She smiled at Tessa's own smile as Thomas latched on more confidently. 'That's much better. He wasn't opening wide enough before.'

In the morning Tessa discovered that one of the women she'd been seeing in clinic for four months had been admitted into the room next to hers.

'Oh hi, Dr Webster!' The younger woman, awake and alert, beamed at Tessa and called out to her when Tessa was making her way on dismayingly-gingery legs past the cubical. 'You're here too,' she exclaimed. 'You must have been early as well.'

'Two weeks.' Tessa remembered that on Lucy's last visit to see her in clinic they'd calculated that their due dates were within two days of each other. 'And you've had the twins.' She ventured into the room before she realised that there was only one baby in the crib. She stilled. 'Lucy?'

'His brother's OK,' Lucy explained quickly. 'But he was smaller and they decided to keep him in the Baby Unit overnight. I had to have an emergency Caesarean,' she added. 'I went into labour normally but when I came in Mr McEwan examined me and said the cord was in the wrong place. He was worried it would cut off the blood to one of the babies and I had to have the operation straight away. There wasn't time for the epidural because the anaesthetist had to put me to sleep immediately.'

Nathan had had a busy night, Tessa registered. Her nurse had mentioned there'd been two emergency Caesarean sections overnight along with one breech delivery which he would have had to supervise.

At Tessa's inquiring look Lucy continued, 'I didn't mind about missing out on being awake. Not when it was for the sakes of the babies.'

'This one's absolutely gorgeous.' Tessa bent over the sleeping infant. He had a shock of fine dark hair and was smaller than Thomas and less rounded but that was normal given Lucy had been nurturing two babies. 'How are you feeling?'

'Like someone's driven a bus through my insides,' the other mother admitted ruefully. 'What about you?'

'Sore,' Tessa admitted. Nowhere near as sore as she would have been after surgery, but she was still suffering. 'My back aches as much as it did when I was pregnant. I thought I'd spring back like a jack-in-the-box and I was planning to be back at work in a month but at this rate it's going to be two at least before I can walk properly again.'

'I know how you feel.' The other woman laughed. 'I was the same after my first. You're not really going back in four weeks are you?'

'I've allowed myself six,' Tessa conceded. Her employment contract entitled her to twelve weeks' leave without pay but that was a long time to be without an income and also she didn't feel it was fair to place such an extra burden on her colleagues who were covering her work. No one appeared to mind and Nathan, certainly, had done his best to encourage her to consider taking even another three months off, but financially and career-wise that wasn't a reasonable option.

'The hospital has an excellent crèche,' she explained. 'And I'll be starting off only part-time until Thomas is six months.' Child-care was partially subsidised for employees at the new hospital and the standard of care was said to be superb. She'd only ever be a few minutes away from Thomas and she was hoping to be able to continue breastfeeding. The situation wasn't ideal, she hated the idea of leaving her son even for three days a week while he was so young, but then nothing about anything lately had seemed ideal, and her choices were limited. She had to earn a living. Simon was travelling, not working, and until he was settled again, perhaps years from now, she wouldn't be able to rely on him to contribute to Thomas' care.

Lucy said, 'I'd like to go back to teaching one day. But probably not until these two are three. We'll end up relying on our mothers. Families are a lifesaver when it comes to kids, aren't they?'

Tessa smiled and nodded, although the reality was she had no personal experience. Her parents along with her only sister Trudy had drowned in a boating accident when she was in her first year at university and she had no close relatives.

Simon had been alone too. Not because of death, in his case, but divorce. She was always interested in people's families and she'd managed to prise out the details of his on one of their early dates. Simon's father had remarried and had a second family and then a third and he lived in Europe. His mother lived in Auckland. She'd remarried twice too. Simon had disliked his first stepfather and he abhorred his second. He refused to have anything to do with him and as a result, outside of the large cheques that appeared each Christmas and birthday, he had very little contact with his mother.

Despite Simon's deliberate casualness she'd known she'd found a kindred spirit. She'd understood the sense of isolation and loss hidden behind Simon's easy manner and charming smiles because she too was used to living with the constant pain of grief and loneliness.

She'd asked Simon to let his parents know there was going to be a baby but although a company cheque had turned up with a signed card from his father, followed quickly by another cheque from his mother, neither parent had asked to meet her, or her baby, when he or she was born.

Tessa had been stunned by that but Simon had shrugged. The tragedy in her life had left her hungry for human warmth and emotional security and she'd always known she wanted children so that one day she'd once again have a family of her own to love. In contrast, Simon's isolation from his family had made him wary of intimacy and responsibility. The lonely adolescent she saw so poignantly staring out of his adult eyes, the one who'd longed desperately for his parents and stepbrothers and sisters to notice him, had evolved into an adult who spurned what he termed the 'suffocating boredom' of family life and who claimed no interest in becoming a father.

Nevertheless, she intended sending letters and photos of Thomas to Simon's parents now. She was going to try to not get her hopes up too much, on Thomas' behalf, that either of them might want to be involved in his life.

She looked up and smiled as Nathan and two of the department's junior doctors walked into the ward. Her private specialist had already been in to see her earlier that morning and she guessed he'd gone off to his rooms for the morning because Nathan was obviously in charge of the ward round.

'Hi!' He smiled back at both her and Lucy. After a seventy-two-hour duty weekend like the one Tessa knew he'd had she'd have been ragged and exhausted but Nathan looked fresh and immaculately groomed. 'Good night?' he asked.

'Not as busy as yours.' Tessa felt guilty again about being off work. 'I hope you're going to be able to get away early today.'

He didn't answer that. 'How did Thomas sleep?'

'He likes one hour at a time.' She smiled her thanks for the sympathetic sound Lucy made then backed out of the room properly to allow Nathan and the other doctors to move in to see her. 'I'll catch up with you later,' she said, including the other woman and Nathan in that, before leaving them to return to her careful stroll around the perimeter of the ward.

It might be a while before she was back to her usual shape and feeling properly fit again, she acknowledged, deliberately pulling in her belly and straightening her shoulders as she moved. But walking had to be a good start.

She'd settled on a three-day stay in hospital. Karori encouraged early discharge with midwife and specialist-nurse back up and Tessa had expected to want to leave after a day, but this morning the idea of packing and taking Thomas home on her own seemed too scary. A couple more days to improve her feeding technique and to watch how the experts managed Thomas would help her confidence, she hoped.

'I'm useless,' she told Nathan sheepishly when he returned to see her late that afternoon. 'With all my obstetrics training I thought this would all be easy, but it isn't. You should have seen me trying to bath him this morning. It was a disaster. He was petrified.'

Nathan laughed. 'You're exaggerating.'

'I wish I was.' She kept her tone deliberately light although there'd been nothing light about the fear she'd felt at the time. 'I was clumsy as anything. Poor Thomas was convinced I was going to drown him.'

'He doesn't think like that yet,' he argued, smiling down at the baby in his arms.

'His arms flew out,' she told him.

'Sounds like you triggered a normal Moro reflex,' he declared blandly, referring to an instinctive movement in babies where they spread their arms then brought them together again in a startle-response to being tipped.

Tessa still had doubts. 'His left hip,' she said delicately. 'I know I shouldn't worry since you've looked at him and the orthopaedic registrar's looked as well, but when I was changing him before I noticed it seemed a bit clicky.'

'It wasn't when I examined him yesterday.' He sent her a chiding look but to her relief he moved to put Thomas on the bed. With skill commensurate with long experience he unfastened Thomas' nappy, checked his hips, then wrapped him again and picked him up. 'Normal.'

She tilted her head. 'Are you sure...?'

'Completely.' He looked at her. 'Any other problems?'

'Could he be dehydrated? Do you think he's getting enough milk?'

Nathan ran an assessing hand over Thomas' head. 'No. I'm sure he's getting plenty. Yes. Anything else?'

She chewed her lower lip. 'Well, I don't mean to sound neurotic...'

'When you so obviously are.'

Tessa poked out her tongue at him. 'His right foot turns out. Is it too much? Do you think I should ask the orthopod to have another look at him?'

Nathan rolled his eyes but he tugged off the knitted booties the nurses had given her for Thomas and took another look at his little foot. 'Well within normal limits. You know babies often have funny feet. It'll straighten soon enough.'

'But ...'

'Tessa, do us all a big favour and stop examining your own baby.'

'I can't help it,' she confessed. The thousands of babies she must have examined in the past didn't help her when it came to Thomas because with him she seemed incapable of distinguishing between a normal variant and abnormal. 'Last night I sat for hours counting his toes over and over.'

'Counting toes is fine. Every parent counts toes. Keeping your own stethoscope around so you can check his heart hourly for murmurs is definitely neurotic.'

Tessa blushed. 'Who told you?'

'The nurses are a little worried.'

'I'm going to be one of those awful, smothering over-protective mothers, aren't I?'

'No.' The bleep Nathan wore in the pocket of his coat blared and Tessa caught a glimpse of the illuminated number on the side and saw that Theatre was calling him. In smooth, easy movements, he stood and passed Thomas back to her. 'You're going to be a relaxed, sweet dream of a mother,' he murmured, ruffling the top of her head. 'Once you find your feet. Be calm. You look frail and you're still pale. Eat more and rest while you can. You have a beautiful baby and he's perfectly fine.'

Despite her attempts to argue with him, Tessa found Nathan's calm dismissal of her concerns enormously reassuring. Between Thomas' feeds she slept almost soundly that night for the first time in weeks and the next afternoon when Nathan called in after his clinic she greeted him with cheerful nonchalance.

'He's perfectly happy,' she chirped when he peeked over the bassinet at the sleeping Thomas. 'He's been up for a few hours but he's just been fed and put back down again.'

Nathan's green eyes twinkled at her. 'No new ailments?'

'No.' She felt silly. 'Well, he's drowsy all the time and he does keep dropping off to sleep but everyone tells me to be grateful. I've had loads of visitors today. Half the Gynae nurses have been up to see him as well as most of the midwives. How are the wards?'

He lifted one broad shoulder. 'Same as usual.'

'What about antenatal clinic yesterday? The nurses mentioned you had to add a few emergencies. Did you manage to get away on time?'

'More or less.' From the briefness of his responses she guessed he didn't want to talk to her about work, at least not while she was supposed to be on leave, and so she let the subject drop.

She saw his eyes track to the flowers along the windowsill. People had been very kind and she'd been given lots of flowers and pot plants along with presents for Thomas. But instead of noticing that she'd managed to rescue his Christmas lilies, the ones he'd thrown out the door, Nathan's gaze zeroed in on the dozen yellow roses Simon had sent her. 'Still planning on going home tomorrow?'

'In the morning,' she confirmed. Her gaze skittered to her side table and the brisk, painfully-impersonal note of congratulations – as if he were a distant acquaintance, not the man who'd shared her life for three years and had fathered Thomas – that had accompanied the roses before returning to meet Nathan's enigmatic regard. Trying to make the gesture seem casual, she turned the card over so only the florist's label was obvious. It wasn't that she expected Nathan to try and read Simon's note, it was simply that she didn't want him to see the words accidentally because she didn't want him to start worrying about her again.

'I think I'm ready to go home tomorrow now.' It was lovely being looked after and having her meals delivered and having help with Thomas, but it was time to face reality. 'I can't wait to see how Thomas likes it in his new nursery.'

'You're feeling more confident today then?'

'Getting there.' She didn't feel completely in command yet but at least now she could envisage a time when she might. 'It's amazing what a few hours of good sleep can do for you. I even managed to bath him without shaking too much. But one of the midwives will call in to see me and the nurses will be around to visit Thomas so I'll have plenty of support if I need it.'

'How are you getting home?'

'I thought a taxi.' She saw his frown and added defensively, 'At least that'll mean I can be flexible on the timing. I won't worry I'm holding someone up if I'm not ready exactly on time.'

'You're not going home from hospital with your first baby alone and in a taxi,' he said disapprovingly. 'What about the stairs?'

'I have no choice and I'm sure the driver will help.' From the living room of the house she was renting in Aro Valley, a picturesque, vaguely bohemian area not far from central Wellington, she had glorious bush views, but the down side was difficult access from the road below. There were fifty-six steep cement and stone steps leading up to the house from street level and another short flight inside from the entrance area up to the main living room and bedrooms. 'Stop feeling sorry for me. I might have struggled a bit getting up and down the last month or so of being pregnant but I'll be fine now,' she assured him heartily.

Struggle was an understatement. During the last three weeks of her pregnancy, getting up to the house had meant several stops on the way and a good ten minutes to recover at the top. But now she'd had Thomas she didn't think she'd have too much trouble. 'The exercise will be good for me.'

'Not if it kills you.'

'Which I suppose is your nice way of saying I'm still shaped like a beach ball,' she complained. 'I realise I probably look grossly obese, Nathan, but I think I can manage a step or two without actually bringing on a heart attack.'

'You know I didn't mean that.' He was still disapproving. 'I'm saying that I still think it would be a good idea if you and Thomas come and stay with me for a while.'

Tessa sighed and smiled at the same time. She reached up and touched his cheek briefly but fondly. 'Thanks but no thanks.' They'd discussed this several times. He'd recently moved into a large timber pole home he'd had designed and built high up on a hill in Khandallah, one of Wellington's poshest suburbs. He had dramatic bush and city and harbour views and an enormous heated swimming pool along with perfect access with a driveway and carport close to the front door of the house. It was a beautiful home, but it was his home, not hers, and it didn't matter how many times he offered her a place to stay, she wasn't going to take advantage of his kindness. 'You're too generous for your own good,' she chided. 'The stairs are fine and even if they weren't we wouldn't dream of inflicting ourselves on you like that.'

'It's not *genorosity*.' His green regard turned impatient. 'You know I want to help.'

'You've already been fantastic. I don't know how I would have managed without you these past few months. But you don't have to spend the rest of your life making up for Simon. I know he's your friend but you don't have to take responsibility for us.'

'You've forgotten,' he countered heavily. 'There's a good reason why I am responsible. If I hadn't introduced you to Simon, Tessa, you wouldn't be in this position now.'

chapter three

Nathan's claim was so ridiculous that Tessa started laughing. It had never occurred to her that he might feel any obligation because of Simon's behaviour, but suddenly his concern made perfect sense. 'You poor thing,' she managed finally. 'I can't believe you feel guilty about that. I was happy with Simon. I don't regret the time we had together. And trust me, if it hadn't been him, it could have been someone much worse.'

That wasn't so unlikely. When it came to men, her judgement had never been good. She invariably fell for the good-looking, commitment-phobic, break-your-heart, love-you-and-leave-you type. She never saw the danger at first because the little-boy-lost look always fooled her.

Which meant that instead of the husband and family and settled, homely home life she'd expected to have long before now, here she was, somehow, a twenty-seven-year-old, insecure, unmarried mother who was going to have to juggle raising her only son with the full-time demands of her career.

Only William and Simon seemed to prove that her instincts hadn't necessarily improved in recent years either. She'd almost married William and he'd hurt her a lot. Perhaps because she'd trusted him so completely that she hadn't heeded the warning signs. With other men she would have known she was taking a risk calling on them unexpectedly, but the thought hadn't even occurred to her with her fiancé. Until one night after hours at his surgery, calling in to surprise him with a hot meal, she'd discovered his receptionist busy with a task that William had always been fond of but one Tessa was confident wasn't included in the poor girl's job description.

Even for her that had been too much. The receptionist, her face the colour of a beetroot, had scrambled to her feet and fled the room, but William, casually zipping himself up, had acted as if he'd been caught out in a minor indiscretion which, he claimed, had nothing to do with how much he loved her.

Tessa had removed her ring by then and as William started to realise that she was serious, he'd grown angry. He'd shouted about the money they'd spent on the arrangements and the deposits and her promise to pay back half of the expenses hadn't mollified him. His final words, when he pursued her to the car park, were that he was relieved it was over because she'd never performed the act with the same eagerness as his receptionist and he must have been an idiot to even consider marrying a woman who hated sex.

That had shaken her. Even through the pain, his sensitivity had astounded her. She'd always thought she was pretty convincing in that area and nobody else had ever guessed her enthusiasm wasn't genuine.

Not that he was right about everything. She didn't *hate* sex. True, she was never driven mad with lust, nor did she thrash about in a wild passion having multiple orgasms every night of the week – although until William she'd thought she was brilliant at pretending she was doing both those things – but then how many women really did react that way?

William's insight though had forced her to confront her sexual inadequacies and she'd made a vow to herself that with the next man, if there ever was one – at that stage she'd been devastated enough to doubt it – she would be honest. If he couldn't love her for the way she was, then that was that.

Then Nathan introduced her to Simon. From the start he'd felt special, she'd felt that the bond between them was special, and although she'd wanted, desperately, not to deceive him, in the end she hadn't been able to hurt him by revealing that his attempts to arouse her were in vain. And by then she hadn't wanted to lose him.

The end result was that they'd had a lot of happy times together. She'd thought she'd found the right man at last. She'd been overjoyed that she'd broken a pattern of destructive relationships and that she'd finally found someone with whom she could share her life. She'd loved him. She'd assumed that Simon, in his own way, had loved her in return.

Which he had, he'd protested. Just not enough to commit the rest of his life to her when the contraception she'd always fitted so diligently had one day failed.

From the start the thought of a baby had filled her with joy, but Simon had panicked. He'd seen only the sacrifices he'd have to make if he opted for domesticity.

It hadn't been an easy time for her but that was behind her now, she told herself firmly. There was no point in looking back and having regrets and berating herself for her inadequacies because that only brought the whole awful mess back to the front of her mind and made it hurt all over again. She reminded herself that she was going to be strong.

'Even if things didn't work out like a fairy tale happily ever after,' she gazed at her son as she spoke to Nathan, 'Simon gave me Thomas. He's the best thing that's ever happened to me. And I'm grateful,' she told her colleague sincerely, 'for your offer. Truly. But we'll be happy in our own home and the steps will be fine.'

'Stay till six tomorrow night so I can drive you home after work.'

'They need my bed first thing.'

'Then let me at least arrange someone else to drive you.'

She tilted her head. 'Who?'

'Never mind who. Someone. All right?'

Tessa really didn't mind about the taxi and she was tempted to argue again, or go ahead and order a cab anyway, but Nathan had been so good to her that she didn't want to offend him and it was obviously important to him and so she nodded acquiescence.

In the morning she half-expected him to get back to her to explain that he hadn't been able to find anyone who could get away from work for the time it would take to drive her and Thomas home, but she should have realised he'd not let anything stand in his way because he arrived shortly after eight. With his parents.

'Tessa, you remember Mum and Dad, don't you?'

'Of course.' Tessa had been up since six, she'd fed and changed and dressed Thomas and packed and even found time to smear on some lipstick, and she rose from the chair in which she'd been sitting with her son to greet the beaming couple. She'd met Nathan's parents several times — Simon knew them well since he'd spent school holidays with Nathan's family when he was a child — and she'd seen them most recently at Nathan's housewarming for his new home. She remembered they ran a farm near Palmerston North, two and a half hours' drive north of Wellington. 'This is a surprise. Hello.'

'Hello, Tessa dear.' Nathan's mother kissed her cheek.

'Oh, he's gorgeous,' she cooed, bending back the cotton blanket Tessa was holding Thomas in to smile at his pink little face. 'You were right, Nathan, he's absolutely beautiful. Hello, Thomas. He has your chin, Tessa.'

'Yes, poor creature,' Tessa recited mildly. Several visitors had already pointed that out. 'Luckily he takes after Simon in most other things so far. Apparently he was a small baby too but I was a ten pound dumpling for my poor mother.'

Nathan's mother exchanged an unreadable look with her son then said lightly, 'Well you're certainly not a dumpling now. No one would guess you've just had a baby,' she added. Tessa knew that was a huge lie but she smiled to thank her for her kindness and the older woman smiled back and her sparklingly-vivid green eyes, the image of Nathan's, flickered in his direction again. 'Nathan was less than six pounds. The doctors were worried he was too small. You wouldn't believe it to look at him now.'

'You wouldn't,' Tessa agreed. She met her colleague's weary roll of his eyes with an exaggerated eye roll of her own. Nathan was around six feet and his broad shoulders and athletic build and dark good looks contributed to him being considered one of the hospital's heart-throbs.

Technically, Simon, with his boyish charm, gleaming blond hair and incongruous chocolate brown eyes, probably came out ahead on looks. But Simon preferred to skim breezily the emotional surface of life. Nathan's depth, his self-assurance and warmth and his understated emotional strength, in contrast, were powerfully compelling.

Not that Nathan ever took advantage of his appeal. He got offers all the time, she knew, yet he rarely dated.

He took his responsibilities seriously and she guessed, from the little she'd been able to prise out of him with her teasing about the abysmal state of his love life, that he'd made a deliberate decision that his career would be his priority until after he became a specialist.

She understood that. Registrars had to work long hours on site at the hospital but as specialists they'd be able to cover a lot of that on-call work from home, reducing their total hours. Life as a registrar with a family was usually a complex balancing act between time at work and time with a family. Invariably, doctors made compromises. She was going to have to deal with that conundrum in her own life. Nathan, she suspected, wouldn't find compromise acceptable in his.

She hoped that didn't mean he was lonely.

'I'm due in surgery,' he said definitively then. 'Tess, you'll be all right then?'

'I'm sure I will.' Tessa smiled her thanks to his parents once Nathan had nodded brisk farewells and left them. 'This is incredibly kind of you. I don't know how to thank you. I'm ready to go if you are. I hope Nathan didn't bully you too much.'

'Oh, it's no trouble, lass.' Nathan's father was still beaming. 'We're going to an auction in Wellington today so you're not out of the way at all. That's a good-looking boy you've got there.'

'That's the Simon in him,' she agreed, gazing down at Thomas. Thomas' eyes were still blue, like hers, but since in almost every other way he resembled Simon, she was expecting them to turn dark brown in time.

'I'll take this then, shall I?' Nathan's mother collected the bag containing Tessa's toiletries from the end of the bed along with the flowers she was taking home and a few odds and ends. 'And I'll take the capsule,' she added, picking up the baby car seat the nurses had arranged for Tessa to hire temporarily until he was a little bigger when she'd buy her own. 'Bill, you bring Tessa's big bag and Thomas' things. It's sunny but there's a stiff breeze out there, Tessa, are you going to be warm enough?'

'I've got a cardie,' Tessa explained, grabbing it from the end of the bed before she followed them out. The hospital seemed always to be heated, even in summer, and after four days she was looking forward to fresh air again, even if that meant facing one of Wellington's legendary winds. She'd already said her good-byes to the staff on the ward but she called in at the main nursing station on her way past to say she was going.

'Take care, Tessa. It's been lovely having you both.' Claire, the midwife who'd been with her for Thomas' delivery, smiled down at Thomas and touched his cheek with one knuckle. 'And you look after your mother, young man. She's very precious. Don't you wear her out. We need her back at work here fit and well ASAP.'

'Six weeks,' Tessa promised, crossing her fingers.

Thomas seemed content strapped into his little harness and Nathan's mother insisted Tessa sit in the front seat of their four wheel drive so she'd be less cramped than in the back. The other woman climbed sprightly in beside a dozing Thomas then sat forward between the seats and chattered most of the way. Firstly about the weather and what a good summer they were having and then the farm and then about Nathan's older brother, Jack, who was working in Toronto but had recently been back to New Zealand and was hoping to return for good later in the year. He'd been offered a locum appointment at The Starship Hospital, a specialist children's hospital, in

Auckland, New Zealand's largest city.

'It will only be short term unfortunately,' she told Tessa. 'The usual consultant's going on sabbatical leave to the hospital Jack's working at now in Canada. Jack's hoping it might lead to a permanent position eventually though.'

Tessa mentioned that there was talk at Karori hospital about funds being approved for a new children's doctor position towards the end of the year. She'd never met Nathan's brother but she knew he was well known and highly respected in his field. 'Would Jack consider working down here?'

'He might,' Nathan's mother said slowly. 'And that way we'd get to see him more often than once or twice a year. We'll mention it to him.'

'It's seems funny that you're both farmers yet all three of your children have become doctors,' Tessa observed. Nathan's sister Zoe had graduated at the end of the year and was now doing her internship at Wellington's main hospital in the city. 'How do you think that happened?'

'Bill's father was the local GP for thirty years,' Nathan's mother explained, nodding to her husband. 'We suspect seeing him in that job had an effect on them when they were younger.'

'Nathan's the only one who always wanted to be a doctor, mind,' her husband countered with a wink at Tessa. 'He's been sure of that all his life. He was always first in line to follow Dad around on his rounds. Zoe was going to be a vet at first, then she decided she was going to join the circus before settling on acting. It was only when she finished school with good marks that she decided to follow the boys into medicine.' The pair exchanged smiles and Tessa got the feeling they remained bemused by their youngest child's final choice.

'Jack always liked action,' Nathan's mother added. 'He wanted to be in the airforce but by that time he was ready for university he'd settled on getting his pilot's license as a hobby but studying medicine for his career. But he's good with children and he's very happy in paediatrics.'

'Does he have a family of his own?'

Nathan's father grinned. 'He's never been in any hurry to settle down. Not often we see him with same girl twice. Although we do sometimes see him with two at once.'

Tessa smiled. 'They're all different, aren't they? Zoe, so…' she wanted to say 'dizzy' or 'flighty' which would have been accurate considering what she knew of Zoe but she was worried that might offend them and so she searched for something less emotive, '… so flamboyant,' she said instead. 'Jack obviously so adventurous and Nathan so calm and sensible.'

'Nathan's certainly the quietest of the three. Jack and Zoe were like little firecrackers when they were young, running around getting into mischief if I turned my back for five minutes unless Nathan was there to keep them out of trouble. If he was with them, I didn't have to worry so much.'

Tessa laughed. 'He'd give them a good telling off if they were naughty I imagine. He used to do the same to me when I first started working with him. He thought I wasn't taking my career seriously enough.'

She'd never consciously planned a career in O and G. She'd drifted into it because when the time had come for her to have to make a choice, there'd been a vacancy on the rotation. A couple of times in the early years she'd considered dropping out and maybe going into a less arduous field, but Nathan, impatient with her haphazard decision making, had talked her out of it each time. She had a gift for obstetrics, he'd told her. One she'd be stupid to throw away.

She realised now that of course it was the perfect speciality for her. In medicine and general surgery she'd had to deal with grief and despair almost on a daily basis and she'd found that difficult emotionally. Obstetrics was biased towards the happy side of human existence.

'He's a very calming influence.' She couldn't think of anyone she'd rather have around in an emergency. 'I like Nathan. I like him very much.' In the heated and sometimes panicky chaotic atmosphere of hospital practice, there'd been times when she'd felt he was keeping her sane. 'He's a fantastic doctor and a wonderful surgeon and his patients adore him. You must be very proud of him.'

'We are.' His mother smiled. 'We're proud of all our children.'

Tessa showed them where to park on the street beneath the steps but she didn't want them to feel obliged to come up. 'Leave everything down here,' she instructed hastily, when they began unloading her little collection of belongings. 'I'll take Thomas up first and settle him in then come back down for the rest. You must be in a hurry to get on.'

'No hurry at all, lass.' Nathan's father eyed the steps then, apparently undaunted, he collected two bags and regarded her blandly. 'We don't have to be in town till eleven. Don't worry about us, we're fit as fiddles. These few bags aren't much compared with the weight of a sheep. Shall I take the boy or would you prefer to carry him yourself?'

'I'm fine with him.' But the combined weight of Thomas and his capsule was enough for her to decide to carry them separately and she unclipped her son and lifted him out.

Nathan's father scooped up the cradle and her toiletry case and followed her, his wife coming behind with Thomas' blanket and Tessa's handbag and the plants and Simon's roses.

Dismayingly, Tessa found she had to stop twice on the way up and she was breathing hard when she finally let them into the house. It was musty after her days away so she left Thomas with Nathan's mother and hurried about opening doors and windows to the breezes.

'Excuse the mess,' she apologised, waving her arms at all the discarded books and papers. 'I was trying to study when I first went into labour but when the pains started getting bad I couldn't face cleaning up.' She put water on to boil. 'Tea?'

'It's very peaceful.' Both nodded their desire for a drink and Nathan's mother, still holding Thomas, wandered over to the far window and looked out over Tessa's lawn and vegetable garden to the bush beyond. 'You'd never know you're only five minutes from the city. You obviously have green fingers, Tessa. Nathan's house will look much better once he finds time to get a garden in.'

'I love gardening,' she confessed. 'Unfortunately, despite all the work I've done, I suspect I'm not going to be able to stay here much longer. My lease is almost up and there's been no mention of a renewal. The landlady came to take photos of the house recently and I think she's considering selling.'

'You couldn't buy it yourself?'

'Sadly no.' She'd like to – she'd *love* to – but without Simon helping financially, the premium price the old house would demand would be beyond her budget. In five years she might be able to afford a deposit on a home with similar charm, but she had Thomas to think about now. She didn't need to panic, she had savings and her income would increase in future once she qualified as a specialist, but for now she needed to take care and it wasn't the right time to be committing herself to huge mortgage payments.

She liked baking but she hadn't had a lot of time or energy lately and the only biscuits she had in the house were store bought ones. She served a packet for morning tea and when they'd finished most of them and their drinks, Nathan's mother said they had to be going.

'Thank you so much,' she said, following them outside to the top of the steps. 'You've been very kind. I didn't think I'd mind coming home alone but it's been lovely having company for this first time.'

They both beamed at her but Nathan's mother squeezed her arm. 'We've enjoyed ourselves. It's been lovely being able to hold a baby again. Thomas is beautiful, dear. Really beautiful.'

'I expect it won't be that long before you have grandchildren of your own,' Tessa assured her. 'Nathan's too lovely to stay single for long once he decides he's ready for a family and there are a couple of women at work who'd fall over themselves to go out with him if he paid them any attention.'

'Oh, I have a feeling he's already found the one he wants,' the older woman countered lightly. Her eyes very green now she smiled at Tessa then kissed her cheek. 'Knowing Nathan, I suspect he's biding his time until the moment's right. Goodbye, dear. All the best. Hopefully we'll see you and Thomas again soon. You must come up to the farm.'

'And you should come for tea,' Tessa called after them.

'Next time you're down. Drop in any time.' She stood at the stop of the stairs, watching them go and pondering Nathan's mother's mystery revelation. The older woman had sounded very confident and Tessa found it hard to doubt her. She wondered who'd attracted Nathan's interest.

chapter four

Nathan called by after six. She'd wondered if he might and she wasn't surprised to hear footsteps on the steps outside. 'Surviving?' he asked, coming up stairs and leaning in her open doorway to smile at her where she stood washing tomatoes for her tea.

'Of course. Oh a Teddy bear,' she exclaimed, wiping dry her hands then taking the fluffy brown-eyed creature he'd been holding behind his back. 'He's beautiful. Thank you. Thomas will love him. And you're not even puffing,' she accused, wrinkling her nose. Clutching the bear, she went up onto tiptoes to exchange kisses. 'How could you climb all the way up here and not be puffing? You must have stopped for a rest.'

'Poor baby.' He grinned. 'A struggle, was it?'

'You were right about me not being fit,' she confessed. 'The top stretch almost killed me. Your parents must have been worried because they stayed for morning tea when they were probably in a hurry to get into town. How was work?'

He lifted one broad shoulder. 'As always.'

'I keep forgetting to ask you about Ellen.' Tessa sat the bear on a chair and moved automatically to fill the kettle. Ellen Wentworth was a thirty-year-old woman in her first pregnancy who'd developed early signs of raised blood pressure and leg swelling. The only cure was to deliver the baby but since Ellen's due date was eight weeks away Tessa had admitted her to try and make sure she rested. They were hoping to be able to delay the birth until her baby had more time to develop. 'How's she doing?'

'Marginal.' He waggled his hand in the air to indicate that their patient's medical state was delicately balanced. 'She's well but we may not get away with delaying things much longer.'

'I'll keep my fingers crossed.' Tessa switched off the power and added the boiling water to the pot she'd prepared. 'Is she coping?'

'Only by driving everyone else crazy.'

Tessa nodded sympathetically. She understood why the other woman might be frustrated about the enforced rest. Ellen was a dynamic woman who held down a high-powered marketing career in the city and was also strongly involved in both community work, sport coaching and local and regional-level politics. When Tessa had told her she needed to come into hospital, Ellen had been appalled. She'd expected pregnancy to fit in with her lifestyle just as everything else did, and the fact that things weren't going as smoothly as she intended had come as a shock to her.

'I suppose she's still got her laptop installed along with the two mobile phones,' she offered.

'And the rest.' Nathan rolled his eyes. 'Yesterday I ordered her to tone down the work but she's had a secretary in there half the day today along with a portable copier machine and a second line connected to the Internet and a fax. There've been deputations from the council and the netball team she coaches has been in this afternoon to get tips for their pre-season training schedule. I've told her if she doesn't settle down I'll put her in isolation for a week.'

Tessa grimaced. 'Is her husband coping?'

'He's thrilled.' Nathan took the mug of tea she passed

him. 'He loves having her confined on the ward. They've been married six years and it's the first time he's seen her more than one night a week.'

'I hope she'll be all right. She's in the right place at least if you need to operate immediately.' She followed Nathan over to the armchairs by the window, put down her mug on the low table between them, then supported her lower back with one hand as she sat down.

'Back hurting?'

'It aches a bit from time to time.' She grimaced. 'I spent an hour gardening this afternoon and I've stirred things up. But I'm fine. Really.'

'You didn't look fine when you sat down just now. Would a massage help?'

'If that's an offer, then yes please.' Nathan was an expert. He taught classes in baby massage at the hospital and the last time they'd gone skiing with a group from the hospital her back had been so sore the morning after the first day that she'd barely been able to get out of bed. Simon had been too eager to get out onto the slopes to help her but a twenty-minute massage from Nathan had been enough to free her up for the new day. 'But I don't want to put you to any trouble...'

'Stand up.' He cut off her protests. 'Let me examine you.'

He took her hand and helped her up, then turned her so she faced away from him. She felt his hand spreading against her lower back. 'Bend forward. As far as you can.' He made her move every way possible, checking that she had a full range of movement.

'Do you have oils?'

'Sesame or olive?'

'That's it?'

'Sorry.' She laughed at his perplexed expression. 'I can tell by your face that the women you're used to have bathroom cabinets full of massage oils and scented candles. Sorry. Mine's full of old make-up and spare toilet paper and chocolate in case I get hungry in the bath. I'll go for the olive. It's supposed to be good for your skin and I bought an extra bottle a month ago so I've more of that.' She felt guilty but the idea of one of Nathan's massages was too tempting to resist. 'You finish your tea while I'll get towels.'

She collected together the oil and plenty of towels and a pillow and when she came back he was rolling up his shirtsleeves. They decided the sofa was too narrow so he helped her spread the towels across the carpet. She left her shirt on and lay on her front and she hitched up her skirt and gathered it at midriff level and tucked it under. Her knickers were the sort that came up in a broad inverted triangle to a band at her waist and she folded them down over her buttocks to expose her lower back.

'Too far.' Warm fingers restored her underwear to full stretch with a snap of elastic. 'You're pushing the friendship boundaries with that one, Tessa.'

'Chicken.' She turned her head to look at him where he knelt at her side. 'Hey, come on,' she protested at the stern look the comment earned her. 'You've known me so long we're like brother and sister and four days ago you helped me give birth. Don't tell me the sight of my half-naked bum can still frighten you after that.'

'I'm not frightened.' He placed a folded towel over her offending anatomy. 'But you're not my sister and this is meant to be therapeutic, not erotic. We don't want any distractions here.'

'Mmm, sure. Erotic.' Tessa smiled into her pillow. 'Like

you could even for one second lust after my bottom.'

'You don't think so?' He sounded thoughtful. She heard him opening the oil then seconds later he ran the heels of his hands down her spine. His fingers spread beneath the towel in a firm, dual-handed motion. 'I would say that what I saw looked fairly tempting.'

As if. More likely it was fairly dimpled, Tessa knew. She hadn't exactly had time to over-indulge on the exercise front over the past year. But it was kind of Nathan to pretend and she stretched out with a sigh. 'You say the sweetest things.' She closed her eyes and after a little while his warm, oil-moistened hands shifted rhythm to move in deep, tension-draining circles across her lower back. 'But don't worry, it won't go to my head. I promise not to throw myself at you. This week, at least.'

He made a small, amused sound but he didn't say anything. He switched from circles to long, firm strokes along her spine and she let her head sag into her pillow and sighed again with bliss, relaxing, slowly, as for the first time in days, her pain began to melt away.

'You are amazingly good at this,' she told him eventually. 'How long did you train for?'

'Over a year part time while I was at varsity. I did the course with a friend.'

'A girlfriend I bet,' she commented drowsily. She remembered his comment about erotic massage and felt her colour flutter a little. Too much knowledge, she thought wryly. She wasn't used to thinking of Nathan in a sexual context. But still…now he'd forced that image upon her she admitted being mildly intrigued. 'How could she bear to let you go?'

His hands tightened fractionally at her hips. 'You can't relax and talk at the same time.'

Tessa moved her arms out from her sides and folded them under her pillow and rested her head back down. She tried to relax her mind but her curiosity was too aroused. 'So tell me, what do you do with an erotic massage? Does it mean sex after a back rub? Or is it that the massage itself is kinky?'

She was aware of him moving to kneel over her and then the heels of his hands slowly worked their way down from her waist to her buttocks in a warm, soothing motion. 'Kinky?'

'You know.' Sure she was flushing, she was glad he couldn't see her face. 'Genital stuff.'

'I don't think there are rules.'

'Or if there are, you aren't going to tell me them.'

The pressure of his hands on her back muscles eased and for a few seconds his fingers slid across her skin in a movement that was more a caress than a massage. 'How curious are you?'

She giggled. 'Not enough to want to try it out.'

He lowered his head till his mouth almost touched her ear. 'Then shut up,' he growled, his hands pressing deeper again, 'and let me concentrate.'

Tessa smiled. She put her head down and closed her eyes again and gave herself up to the sheer pleasure of the massage.

Too soon, the soft roughness of a towel was opened against her. 'Relax for a minute,' Nathan told her softly. 'I'll fetch a flannel and soap to take off the oil in case it stains your clothes. Sleepy?'

'A little.' But she opened her eyes. 'My back feels wonderful. Hey, Nate?'

He was replacing the lid on the oil when she turned her head. 'Hmm?'

What she wanted to ask was what he'd have said to extract himself if she'd said yes. Before. About trying out an erotic massage. But she looked at him and their eyes met and in the evening light his were far too amused and knowing for her to think she'd come off the victor if she tried to tease him about it and the question faded on her tongue. 'Nothing. Sorry.'

'No problem.' He stayed kneeling for a few seconds. 'I'll get that face cloth.'

He wasn't long. The flannel was warm and she lay quietly while he crouched beside her and soaped her back and then dried her off with a towel. By the time he finished she felt languid and warm and drowsy. 'Thank you,' she murmured. 'That was blissful.' She rolled over slowly and started to get up. 'I feel like a baby now myself.'

'Your top's undone.'

'What?'

It took her a few seconds to realise what he meant and it was only when she followed his gaze down that she realised that the buttons had come open and she was giving him the full, *full*, full frontal.

Nathan had already seen her feeding Thomas and he'd seen far more private parts of her body when she was in hospital, so there was no need for her to feel self-conscious, but still she felt her face and neck flood with colour. 'Whoops!' She half-choked on a nervous laugh and clutched the lapels of her shirt together.' She held the fabric tightly closed over her chest, 'This stupid shirt's as the hills and it's normally loose as anything but with the way I was lying on the floor the buttons must have popped...' She broke off and fumbled with the buttons, trying to hold the front in place with her elbows. The stupid thing was, it was her own fault. She'd bought three new maternity bras but they were all freshly washed and pegged to her washing line. 'New mother lesson number four thousand and one,' she mumbled. 'Always wear a bra. Sorry.'

'It's OK.' He took her spare hand and helped her to her feet. 'My blood pressure might take a few days to get back to normal but I'll live.'

'That's a relief.' She smiled. If he could still tease her, she couldn't have shocked him too much. 'I'd never forgive myself if I gave you a heart attack.'

'There was a good chance. I'd only just recovered from your bottom,' he murmured, straightening her collar. 'Do me a favour next time you're going to show off some spectacular body part, give me a couple of seconds warning, hmm?'

'So you can cover your eyes.'

'Believe that if you need to.' He sounded amused. 'You've got yourself all out of order.' He unfastened the buttons she'd managed and connected them with the holes she'd missed and did her up again in the right sequence. 'It's a pretty shirt. The pink brings out the colour in your cheeks.'

No, embarrassment had done that, she knew, but she thanked him anyway. She stood staring up at him, while he straightened her shoulders expertly then adjusted the hem of the shirt before letting her go. 'You're very thorough. You've done this before.'

It was a silly thing to say because of course he had. He'd probably dressed and undressed loads of woman. He might rate work more highly than his social life these days but he was too attractive not to have had plenty of experience in the past. But he didn't make fun of her. He studied her silently for a few seconds, rather solemnly, she thought, then just as she started to feel tense, he turned away. 'I think Thomas cried out. Want me to check him?'

'I'll go.' Tessa hadn't heard anything but she was suddenly guilty about leaving Thomas on his own for so long. Normally she checked him every fifteen minutes or so, she was still too new and too nervous a mother to leave him alone any longer than that, but the massage had taken at least half an hour. Her skirt was bunched around her hips and she pulled it out to full length and headed across the room, collecting the Teddy on her way.

She'd assumed Nathan would want to stay in the main room and she was surprised when he followed her. It was time she fed Thomas but whatever had woken him couldn't have been serious because he was already asleep again, his eyelashes dark and thick against his silky pale cheeks. As always when she looked at him, Tessa's heart swelled with love. 'He's been very good,' she whispered. 'He hasn't cried once since leaving hospital. He knows he's home.'

She lowered the side of the cot and lifted him and for a few seconds they both stood silently watching him. Tessa glanced up at Nathan beside her and smiled, but then she froze, paralysed by an exquisite, unexpected pang of longing.

She felt her eyes tear up and she blinked and wiped them, then averted her gaze.

'Tessa?' The concern in Nathan's voice told her she wasn't doing a very good job of pretending nothing was wrong. He touched her shoulder but she turned away, cradling Thomas carefully, cross with herself for being so pathetic.

'It's nothing. Sorry.' But he looked so worried she couldn't not have explained. 'I'm stupid, I know, but feeling you standing here with me made me think of how perfect it would have been if Simon could have been here now too to see Thomas like this on his first night home.'

'I'm sorry.'

'It's not your fault I'm an idiot.' Cross with her self-indulgence, she carried Thomas over to the big, wicker rocking chair by the window. It seemed a shame to wake him but her breasts were too sore now to leave him. 'This shouldn't take long,' she apologised, tilting Thomas a little to rouse him. 'He doesn't seem hungry.'

She wouldn't have minded if Nathan had wanted to stay but he went to the door. 'I'll make some tea. How about food?'

'I was thinking tomatoes on toast.'

'Take your time here and I'll make it.'

She'd been right about Thomas not wanting a lot of milk and she put on a maternity bra and changed her shirt before coming back out. Nathan poured a cup of tea for her and passed it to her and he switched on the grill. 'Toast in two minutes,' he promised. 'OK?'

'Fine, thanks.' She felt silly about her emotional moment in with Thomas and she hoped he'd forget it. She took over the preparation of the meal but when the tray was ready he took it from her and carried it over to the coffee table in front of the chairs by the window. Tessa took the shabbiest armchair and curled her legs beneath her. She put a cushion over her tummy and surveyed Nathan over the top of her mug. 'Your mother let slip something intriguing today. She mentioned you have a secret girlfriend.'

'Really?' Nathan selected a grilled sandwich for himself. Unlike her, he took a plate too to catch the crumbs. 'She didn't mention a name, did she?'

Tessa smiled. 'You can't fool me, you know. I'm not at all surprised. You're too lovely to have been allowed to stay unattached so long.' She ate some toast then licked her buttery fingers and dusted off the crumbs. 'You can trust me. I know I talk more than I should most of the time, but I'm not a gossip. I've been trying to think all afternoon who it could be. And then I thought, Deborah Carter.'

'Deborah from Theatres?'

'She's been dropping you enough hints. Did you finally get the message and ask her out?'

'I hardly know her.'

'Claire Davies then. She's always had a thing for you.'

'Claire's like that with everyone.'

'Then it must be Georgette,' she pronounced. He'd dated the GP for a short time a year earlier. When he simply frowned at her, she smiled and nodded anyway and took another slice of toast, half-teasing but a little surer now since he hadn't actually denied it. 'I thought it might be,' she affirmed. 'You always looked good together. I liked her, Nathan. You made a lovely couple. I thought it was a shame when you stopped seeing her. Simon thought she was gorgeous...'

He looked tired. 'Tess...'

'I know, I know, it's none of my business but of course I'm curious,' she interrupted quickly, convinced now that she was right. It was. She put her half-finished toast back onto the plate. Georgette was perfect for him. 'I think it's great that you're in love. It's romantic and you deserve to be happy. There's no reason to make a secret of it, is there?'

'I don't...'

'Want to talk about it,' she interrupted. 'That's OK.' She

took a quick slurp of her tea. 'The two of you are in love but it's early and it's too precious to discuss yet.'

'You're wrong.' Nathan put down his plate, moving his tea to make room. 'You don't understand at all. I haven't seen Georgette in almost a year.'

'Oh, no, you're having problems. I'm sorry. Doesn't she feel ready to commit yet? Are you sure she understands how important she is to you?'

'Stop it.'

'Stop what?'

'You know exactly. How's your back now? Did I help?'

She returned her empty tea mug to the table and cupped her chin in her hands and bent forward and looked right back at him the same, cool way he was looking at her. He didn't look unfriendly, merely wary, but Nathan never discussed his romantic relationships with her and their friendship, based on years of working together and trust and fondness, wasn't so intimate that it involved sharing romantic confidences. 'OK,' she said finally. 'If you insist on changing the subject, I'll wait until you feel ready to tell me. Remember I'm here if you need to talk. My back feels great. Better than it has in weeks. Thank you very much.'

'Any time.'

'You might regret saying that.' She bent forward to help herself to more toast. 'Next time I might ask for the erotic version.'

'Any time.'

She looked up sharply. He was joking of course, as she'd been, she knew that, only he'd said the words slowly and deliberately and he hadn't laughed. The light outside was fading now but light from the lamp behind them and from the side threw the chiselled features of his face into shadow except for the pale, almost opaque flare of his eyes as he met her assessing gaze. She offered a tentative smile but he didn't smile back.

Her heart lurched.

She uncurled her legs fast. Time to move, she told herself flatly. Time to *move*. This was Nathan. She'd had the inevitable crush on him when she'd first started working with him, but that was six years ago now and not once in all that time had he shown any sign of being interested in her. Eventually her feelings had faded. When it came to men she might be a walking disaster zone, but at least, she reflected, she seemed to know her limits. She wasn't about to let her feeble supply of romantic wisdom evaporate now.

Nathan wouldn't realise it but their relationship had become the rock that helped anchor her life. She loved it that she could be herself with him, and that she could laugh and relax and even flirt with him, all the time knowing that he knew her too well to take her seriously. Sex, in one way or another, had spoiled every other relationship she'd had with a man. It was liberating to know that it would never spoil this one.

With a brisk sigh she tipped off her cushion, then collected his empty cup. 'Rest easy, I promise you you're safe from me. Another sandwich?' Deliberately she switched on the main lights. 'I've bacon as well as tomatoes if you want something more solid.'

'Not tonight.' He must have shifted quietly because when she turned around at the kitchen he was behind her. 'I'm worried how you're going to manage the steps. Now you've had a chance to see how bad they are, I want you to reconsider coming to stay at the house. At least for a few weeks until you get your fitness back.'

'No thank you.' She smiled though, again, less tentatively this time, to show how much she appreciated his kindness. 'This is our home and the exercise will do me good. Besides,' she kept her voice light, 'I doubt Georgette would approve of you taking us in. Even fat and burdened with baby, I'm still female and we women can be funny about things like that.'

'You're not fat.'

'I do love you.' He didn't argue about Georgette, she noticed. She went up on tiptoes, intending to kiss him as she normally would, but Nathan tensed and when he withdrew slightly she was forced to fall back onto her feet without making contact. Suddenly awkward, she wasn't sure what to think. 'Take care near the bottom then,' she said, speaking quickly to cover her puzzlement. 'I noticed one of the railings has come loose. Thanks again for Thomas' bear and thanks for coming to see us and thanks heaps for the massage, it was lovely.'

He'd started towards the steps but he stopped then and slowly turned around. 'Tessa?'

'Yes?'

'Don't be too trusting.'

She was mystified. 'About what?'

'About anything.' A tiny moth fluttered in the light above his head and he batted it away with a cupped hand, taking care not to hurt it. 'Me, for a start. Don't make assumptions. I'm on call tomorrow night then off Friday and on for the weekend but if I get a chance I'll call by Friday night. I'm submitting my labour study next week and an extra set of eyes to proof it before I send it would be useful.'

'I'd love to read it.' She breathed out in relief. They were still OK then. She'd wondered just now when he'd avoided her kiss. She'd annoyed him with her teasing about Georgette, she realised. His cryptic remarks were a warning that their friendship didn't mean she could take it for granted that he'd tell her anything. Perhaps things really weren't going well? Perhaps – she felt awful – he was nursing a broken heart and his warning was to tell her to stay off the subject because it was too painful? 'Come for a meal,' she invited. 'I'll make something really special.'

chapter five

Friday was a busy day at work for Nathan. His clinic in the morning was fully booked and, though he'd known how popular Tessa was, the clinic reinforced how missed she was. Claire Davies, Tessa's midwife, was at least the tenth person that day to ask how Tessa was.

'I called in Wednesday night and she looked tired still,' he told Claire, after the clinic when she asked after Tessa. 'I'm going to visit tonight.'

He was aware that he was still uneasy about that. He'd considered staying away for a while, but his concern about how she was coping was stronger than his discomfort about how he'd found himself reacting to her on Wednesday night.

He'd never been indifferent to Tessa but until this year she'd always had William or Simon, and at work, technically, for most of the past six years, he'd been her supervisor. Asking her out would always have raised ethical issues for him. They were on equal footings now professionally, but Tessa trusted him, he knew. She was so at ease with him that he knew it would never occur to her that he might find her sexually attractive. And because there wasn't a grain of artifice in her nature he knew that she'd been teasing, pure and simple, when she'd made that comment about asking for an erotic massage.

He had no doubt that she was genuinely curious. And no doubt at all that she had no idea that that sort of massage was merely an extended, incredibly intimate form of foreplay.

His own response had been simple too. So simple it had been primitive.

In an effort to quieten his conscience, he'd made a token effort to warn her. But he'd known she hadn't understood him and he'd told himself that that wasn't so important because he wasn't going to do anything. Unless he was prepared to take ruthless advantage of their friendship and of her loneliness and dented self-esteem after Simon's desertion, his options were non-existent.

'You know Tessa,' he continued to Claire, 'she won't slow down unless she's forced to.'

'Simon hasn't turned up then?'

'Not so far.' He'd noticed Tessa had installed Simon's roses in her living room but as far as he knew that remained the limit of the other man's contributions – apart from the obvious one – so far.

Claire muttered something uncomplimentary but Nathan didn't add anything. He knew that the midwife, along with everyone else, reacted out of sympathy for Tessa and only wished her the best but Tessa wouldn't appreciate knowing her relationship with Simon was so widely discussed.

'Anything I should know about before I take off?' he asked.

'Nothing for you.' Claire scanned the white-board in front of the desk where the status of each of their patients was listed. 'I'm rostered on all weekend unfortunately. Any chance you'll be around to liven things up?'

'I don't know about livening things up, but I'm on duty from eight tomorrow,' he confirmed.

'Oh, you liven things up.' She fluttered her lashes at him. 'Just being here, you do that. What are the odds of us maybe having a cuddle tomorrow night in your duty room if it's not busy?'

'I'd say they're pretty low.' He tapped her nose. 'Saturday's always busy. But thanks for the offer.'

'Don't look so smug, Nathan McEwan,' she called when he walked away. 'I'll get you one day. No man holds out against me forever.'

'See you in the morning.' Nathan lifted his hand in farewell. He dropped in at home on his way up to Tessa's and collected tools and the paper he'd written for her to proof and he parked on the street behind her little car. He mended the loose rail she'd told him about near the bottom of the steps, checked the rest of the railings to be sure they were solid, then replaced his tools and ran up to the house. As usual her door was open and he knocked and when he didn't get a reply, walked straight in and upstairs through the entry and laundry to her living area.

'Tessa...?' She'd transferred Simon's roses from the china vase they'd been in on his last visit to a cut-crystal bowl now in the centre of the table. Some of the petals were starting to brown and curl at the edges but beside the vase, on the table, she'd placed two perfect blooms carefully between paper sheets within the open pages of an ancient-looking encyclopaedia as if she was about to preserve them. He studied them silently, his mouth tightening fractionally, then he made himself look away. When Tessa still didn't appear, he wandered though her living room and out into her garden. She wasn't there and he came back in slowly. 'Anyone home?'

He heard a grumble then sounds of movement from one of the other rooms. A few moments later Tessa emerged, her hair dishevelled in a cloud around her throat and shoulders and her jeans creased. His gaze dropped to the plaid shirt she wore, buttoned unevenly and half in, half out of her waist band. 'Oh,' she said, staring up at him though bleary eyes. 'Nathan.'

His gut tightened. He knew then that he was in trouble. He'd half convinced himself, between the hospital and here, that Wednesday night had been a fleeting fancy and that he'd be back to normal again as soon as he saw her. But he'd been wrong. Roughly he said, 'You were sleeping. I shouldn't have called out, I should have let you rest.'

'I must have…dropped off.' She looked confused. 'I was feeding Thomas and then…mmm, I put him back in his cot but after that…I don't know any more.' She ran a hand through her hair then looked up at him again. 'I forgot you were coming. Em…' She frowned. 'Oh, tea. You're here for tea.'

'Forget it.' Getting out of here sounded like a good idea. He could control this, he was sure of that. Given time. But she was too sexy right now, all muzzy and soft and confused. She made him think of bed and about maybe coaxing her back into hers and that was *no* good.

He remembered her bottom and her breasts and he found his gaze dwelling too long on her mouth. He took a sharp step back. 'I'll leave you to sleep but this time shut the door,' he ordered, his voice thickened by frustration at his inability to control his thoughts. Access from the road wasn't easy but burglaries in Wellington were common enough for him to have installed an alarm at his own home. 'And lock it. I warned you the other night not to be so trusting. It's not safe to go to sleep with the house wide open.'

She nodded vaguely but when he began to retreat, she started protesting. 'No, I'm sorry. Don't go,' she said roughly. 'I'm awake now.' She came after him and caught his arm and held it and warmth of her sent heat up his arm. 'Stay, please,' she insisted. 'I'll feel terrible if you don't when I invited you. You won't want sandwiches again I expect, but there's pasta in the cupboard and tomatoes ready for picking and the basil's getting out of control in the glass-house so I'll add some of that with some peppers and courgettes. Let me have ten minutes to shower and freshen up and then I'll cook.'

Nathan felt the heat from her hand tracking down into his groin. She was so close he could smell the sweet floral scent of her hair and skin. He saw she was looking at him as if waiting a reply and he tried to think but he was still back a couple of sentences. 'You were planning sandwiches again?'

'Just for once. Well, twice today really. I had them for lunch too. Fish paste and peanut butter. Yummy.'

He knew then that he was staying. She'd had a baby and she was breastfeeding. Paste and peanut butter sandwiches weren't going to give her the nourishment she needed. 'I'll cook,' he told her. 'Take as long as you want in the shower.' If he kept his eyes to himself he would survive, he thought. Maybe. 'I'll listen out for Thomas.'

'Thanks.' She sounded breezy again. 'Look in the top cupboards if there's anything special you want. I don't bother with fancy cooking when I'm on my own but there're loads of different things up there left over from when Simon was here.'

Sure enough, her top shelves were crammed with interesting ingredients. There were cans of foreign fruits and fishes and packets of dried Chinese condiments and mushrooms and bottles of exotic sauces and spices and pickles. He considered, with disapproval, her lower shelves, the shelves he guessed she used more now she was on her own. Along with a dozen cans of beans and almost as many again of ready-prepared spaghetti and sausages in tomato sauce and the basic grocery items, her treasures included two jars of fish paste, two more of a garishly-yellow cauliflower preserve, several bags of mini-sized chocolate snacks, two full boxes of chocolates, three bottles of a chocolate sauce that promised to harden when poured over ice-cream, and around a dozen packets of chocolate biscuits.

She'd always had a sweet tooth – Tessa was the only person he knew who took three spoons of sugar in her tea and the nurses on the wards had learned to hide chocolates from her if they wanted any left for themselves – but he was still shocked by the single-mindedness of her supplies.

She reappeared, looking damp and cool and refreshed and lovely and smelling sweetly of roses, as he was adding pasta to a pot of boiling water. 'Why aren't you the size of a bus?' he asked. 'There're kilos of chocolate in these cupboards.'

She beamed. 'I have incredible self-discipline. If I don't open the packets, I'm fine. Once one's opened, well that's a whole other story.' She padded over to him on bare feet. 'And I've never been a rake, Nathan. I could stand losing a few kilos. You found the tomatoes.'

'There're plenty more ripe ones out there,' he warned. He'd picked the most deeply coloured but the plants were laden with fruit. 'If it stays sunny you're going to have to pick them in the next day or two or they'll be dropping off. You shouldn't lose weight.' She had beautiful feet, he registered, puzzled that he'd never noticed that before. They were small and very neat and her nails were painted a delicate, luscious pink. He thought about tipping her back over the table behind them so he could kiss and suck each tiny toe and he had to pull his thoughts up hard to stop himself going any further. 'You're perfect as you are.'

'Perfectly matronly. I'll pick the spare tomatoes tomorrow and freeze them. They're best if they're blanched first. Or I suppose I could make puree.'

'You're not matronly.' Tessa's ignorance of her own appeal had always bemused him but now, alone apart from her sleeping son and bathed in the romantic intimacy of the pale yellow and rose sunset with him in the state he was in now, driving himself crazy imagining kissing her feet, was not the time for a debate about that.

He swung her a quick look, then turned away fast.

He could have done without the sensual shift of her breasts beneath her dress when she walked towards him.

'I couldn't find Parmesan.'

'Because it makes me retch.' She came around to his other side and wrinkled her little nose at him. 'It's too strong. Simon loves it so I used to use it all the time when he was here, but I had to hold my nose. There's processed cheese in a tube in the fridge if you want.'

He grimaced. 'Let's go non-dairy.' At least tonight she was buttoned up tight, he told himself. Unfortunately the sexy way her dress skimmed her curves didn't do anything extra to help his blood pressure.

'I need to check Thomas,' she told him. 'He's probably hungry. Call me if you need anything.'

Nathan didn't watch her go. He finished tearing the basil for the sauce and added it to the tomatoes he'd already chopped along with the spring onions he'd picked. A psychiatrist would have a field day with him right now, he knew. Part of him even wondered whether he ought to seek out one. Fantasising about sucking Tessa's toes was bad enough, but there had to be something seriously perverted about a grown man envying a tiny baby his access to his mother's breasts.

They ate out on cane chairs on her terrace watching the sunset and for dessert Nathan picked fat, fragrant strawberries direct from the garden. He looked around the yard. 'Who did the lawn?' Simon had never taken any interest in the section and Tessa had always cared for the garden and lawns herself but once her pregnancy had become advanced pushing a mower had become difficult for her. She would have persisted, though, Nathan knew, if he hadn't threatened to tie her to a garden chair unless she let him take over. Only the last two weeks his heavy roster at work had stopped him getting back to keep up the work.

'You're not to worry about them any more,' she informed him. 'Mr Marshall next door wants to do them for now. He retired recently and he's desperate for things to do to keep himself busy and he was very keen. He's going to do all the mowing and I'm going to pay him in veggies because his garden's not big enough to grow his own.' She de-stalked a glossy berry and popped it into her mouth but the fruit burst and she made a surprised sound and collected the drizzle of red juice on her lips with the tip of her tongue.

Nathan looked away sharply. He felt his fingers curl into fists. He wondered if it was possible for a woman to be any more sensual than Tessa. He felt a little as if life had suddenly decided to play a joke on him. A very unfunny joke.

'He's not as precise with the edges as you,' she said with a muffled voice, 'but he does them loads better than I do so I think it'll work out fine. Hopefully whoever moves in here after me will want the same arrangement. I'm going to miss the garden when I leave.'

'Leave?' He was startled enough by that to look back at her. 'Where are you going?'

'Not sure yet.' She wiped her fingers across her mouth and licked away the remains of the strawberry juice then made a wry, shrugging motion with her shoulders. 'I knew the landlady was thinking about selling but the agent brought my notice up today confirming it. She wants to do some renovating before it goes on the market and they want the house empty. Officially they've given me three weeks but really they want me out yesterday if I can manage it. If I can be gone in two weeks they'll refund a full month's rent.'

He was shocked. 'Didn't you explain about Thomas?'

'Part of the problem.' She held up her bare ring finger. 'She came up to take photographs a few weeks ago and noticed my bump and my empty finger. She suddenly realised that instead of a nice lady doctor, she was going to have a solo mother in her house. I wasn't surprised about the notice today.'

'You're kidding.' Nathan was appalled. 'Surely, these days...'

'She's a very proper, middle-aged lady. She lives in her own narrow world and she has fixed ideas. People like that don't change too much. She was shocked. It's not that surprising, I'm shocked too. Ten months ago if you'd told me I'd end up raising a child on my own I wouldn't have believed you. It's not an ideal situation. I love Thomas, but there's no sense in pretending he was a planned baby, because he most definitely wasn't.'

'You haven't done anything wrong,' he said strongly. 'You shouldn't be punished.'

'I had sex.' She bent fluidly and collected their plates.

'I was unmarried and I had sex. That's sin enough in some people's eyes.' She straightened, then held out the plates to collect the last of the strawberry hulls he clutched. She looked tired, he saw. Up close he could see the weary lines beneath the glow. 'Silly thing is, all these consequences for something I'll be quite happy living the rest of my life without. Tea?'

'Please.' Frowning, he followed her inside. 'Was that a joke?'

'About coffee or tea? Well there's hot chocolate or Ribena if you prefer but you don't usually like sweet things…'

'Not about the drink,' he interrupted silkily.

'Oh!' She hesitated a second then frowned. 'Oh, sorry, that was a throwaway comment. I didn't mean to offend you.'

'Offend me?'

'As a man.'

'Meaning?'

She looked at him for a long moment without talking then eventually said quietly, 'Well, I don't mean to give you a complex or anything, Nathan, but not all women find sex as important as men seem to.'

He was still mystified. 'On the other hand,' he pointed out, equally quietly, 'quite a lot of women do.' He shook his head when she opened a packet of biscuits and pushed them in his direction. 'It's natural to lose interest after you've had a baby, but sooner or later you'll experience sexual feelings again.' The irony of him being the one to offer her that reassurance wasn't lost on him but he'd gone far enough now to feel forced to finish. 'You can't write off the rest of your life because of what happened with Simon. Even if you two don't manage to resolve things in the future, there'll come a time when you feel ready to move on.'

'I doubt it. It's not having Thomas, or being sad because Simon left. It's more that in my introspective moments it seems crazy to me that a little thing like sex has had such enormous consequences in my life. Good ones, this time, of course. I don't regret Thomas.'

The water had boiled and she poured a little into the teapot, swirled it around, then discarded the water and spooned tea from a canister into the pot. She went up onto tiptoes to reach the cups down from the shelf above the bench and he started forward automatically to help her but before he got there she'd managed on her own. The exertion of stretching had quickened her breathing a little and he had to drag his eyes away from the mesmerising effect that had on her breasts.

'Are you saying you don't enjoy it?'

'I like the hugging and kissing bit.'

He was still puzzled. 'Nothing else?'

'Nope.'

He started to get concerned. 'Do you mean intercourse? But you must know that not every woman finds that alone satisfying.' When she kept watching him silently he went on less assuredly, 'Or do you mean with men in general?'

'I just don't seem have the right nerves in the right places.'

'You've never had an orgasm?'

'I've sneezed plenty of times.' She sort of smiled and frowned at the same time. 'Especially in spring when my hay fever's bad. People say it's similar.'

'Hardly. I don't believe this.' He stared at her. 'Why haven't you done something?' He was as incredulous now as he was shocked. In Gynaecology clinics he'd referred many women in the past to clinicians who specialised in treating sexual difficulties. But it would never have occurred to him that someone as young and vital and sensual as Tessa could experience problems he commonly diagnosed only in traumatised or older, more inhibited women.

Her innocence made his own higher-than-G-rated thoughts about her lately seem even more sordid than they already did.

'You have got to see a therapist.'

'No way.' She poured the tea and passed him his cup. 'I've never been sexually abused or mistreated!'

Nathan half-choked on the first mouthful of his drink and she rolled her eyes at him. 'Come on, we both know what advice they'll give. I've been referring women to them ever since I started in Gynae and I've read all the books. But that doesn't help, because I don't have a problem with non-sexual touch. You know already that I adore being massaged. And I'm not frigid. I can have sex if I want to. My only problem is that I don't find it remotely stimulating.'

'The idea is that you can control the vibrator, making it unthreatening. Therapeutically it's not a penis substitute, it's more a way of discovering where you're sensitive and what you like.'

'I already know what I like.' She finished the biscuit she'd been eating and wiped her hands and wrinkled her nose at him. 'Thomas. And Chocolate. And gardening. And you. Want another cup of tea?'

'No. Don't write off sex, Tessa. You're too sensual a woman not to be able to respond in the right conditions.' Nathan's opinion of Simon had never sunk so low. 'Even if every sexual partner you've had was ignorant, Simon has no excuse. He's studied anatomy. He should have been able to teach you how to…'

'I doubt it ever occurred to him that there was a problem,' she interrupted. 'Don't blame Simon, it isn't his fault. I wasn't very honest with him. You're the first person I've ever told.'

But Nathan was exasperated now. 'He must have known,' he dismissed. 'There are some things no woman can fake.'

'No there aren't. You've seen that film where the girl's in the restaurant pretending…?'

'Oh, God.' Utterly appalled, he sank back against the wall. 'You don't?'

'It always seems easier.' She smiled a little ruefully and looked up at him. 'I've shocked you, haven't I?'

'Profoundly,' he admitted.

'Only William ever guessed. I was always more careful to hide everything with Simon.' She shook her head as if to clear it. 'Anyway, it doesn't matter any more because no man's going to look at me now.'

But Nathan looked at her. He couldn't help himself. He was looking with frustration admittedly, right at this second, as much as lust, but still he looked at her. 'You keep saying that,' he pointed out, 'but it's nonsense and you know it. When was the last time you walked past any man under sixty without him turning to look at you?'

'Probably the day I turned twenty-two.' But she dimpled at him again. 'But thanks anyway. You're so good for my ego. But for now I don't care that I look frumpy because the only men I want around here are you and Thomas. Well, you until you get sick of us at least. Besides, the future's probably mapped out regardless of what I say. As a single mum I'm no great catch. The days of having to beat off men with sticks, not that I ever had those days, are long gone for me.'

He couldn't imagine anything less likely than him growing sick of Tessa and Thomas and she was wrong about the stick. If it weren't for the pangs from his conscience, he knew it would take a lot more than a lump of wood to keep him away. 'No man who's interested in you is going to think twice about being dad to a great baby like Thomas.'

He could tell from the way she rolled her eyes that she didn't believe him. But Thomas crying out distracted her before she replied. She tilted her head at his tiny call and put the new biscuit she'd chosen down untouched on the counter. 'I'll change him then bring him in here to play. He didn't have a lot of milk before, he might be hungry again.'

Nathan remembered the way she'd looked on his last visit with her shirt open. 'It's time I left.' His professionalism during her delivery and hospital stay had been absolute but he knew there was no way now that he was going to be able to watch her feeding Thomas and not react as a man looking at a woman he desired. 'Thanks for dinner.'

She'd started towards Thomas' bedroom but now she turned back. 'What about your article? I haven't proofed it for you yet.'

'I'll bring it back after the weekend,' he told her, collecting the sheaf of papers from the chair where he'd left them before heading down the steps to her front door.

'What's the hurry?' As he opened the door he heard her laugh. 'Nathan McEwan, are you being frightened off by the thought of a messy nappy?'

Nathan didn't answer. The nappy didn't scare him. But

he was frightened. He didn't kid himself that he had any special expertise or prowess when it came to sex, but he knew what he was doing and he didn't think he'd be easily deceived. What he was afraid of was how tempted he was, after Tessa's revelations, to see how thoroughly her responses had been tested.

chapter six

When Nathan mentioned the following Thursday that he was off duty and available at the weekend if she wanted him to baby-sit while she checked out flats for rent, she looked at him guiltily.

'Would you?' she asked. It had been hot as a furnace for days and she hadn't been looking forward to dragging Thomas about the district trying to keep him cool while she checked out places, but she didn't have the luxury of time on her side. 'I was worrying how he'd cope with it all.' She wouldn't worry at all if he was with Nathan. Nathan had done a year of neonatal paediatrics as part of his obstetrics training and his baby-handling skills were vastly more developed than hers. But she hated the thought that she might be taking advantage of him again.

He kept telling her that he was going to be busy at work and that it might be a week before he could get back and that she should call him if she needed anything, but then he kept arriving unexpectedly every night he wasn't working. He insisted on collecting her grocery shopping for her – she was perfectly capable of dragging the bags up from the car but he didn't believe it – and he didn't often arrive without a new toy for Thomas. She had other friends, other people who'd offered help if she ever needed it, but she would never have asked and so Nathan, who simply arrived without asking and told her off when she tried to stop him doing things, had ended up doing far more than she should have allowed.

'But what about Georgette?' she reminded him. With

all the time he was spending with her and Thomas, he had to be neglecting his social life. 'Surely she's not happy about you coming here so often?'

'I'm not seeing Georgette.'

'Because you're here!' Tessa made a face at him. She was certain she was on the right track with her suspicions about the attractive GP. She did feel a little wistful about it, she knew, but that was selfish and silly and just because he was kind enough to help her out, didn't mean she had any right whatsoever to feel possessive about him. He deserved to be happy. She *wanted* him to be happy. 'I know you don't like me talking about her, but be reasonable, Nathan. She must mind at least a little bit.'

'You're mad.' He dealt her a flat look then when Thomas started to cry seconds later he followed her though into his room. 'So what time tomorrow? Ten too early?'

'You're an angel,' she murmured, vowing to make him a very nice lunch to make up for the babysitting. 'Ten's perfect.' In the two to three hours Thomas was lasting between feeds, if she organised appointments in advance she could probably see loads of properties instead of the two or three per day she'd been managing with Thomas with her. 'Thank you.'

She picked Thomas out of the cot and smiled at him. 'I'll take my mobile with me so you'll be able to call me home if you need to. Are you hungry, little man?' She checked his nappy with her palm and it was dry. 'I think you must be, mustn't you?' She gathered him under one arm and carried him out into the living area. 'Are you still doing Ellen Wentworth's Caesarean tomorrow, Nathan, or are you going to try and wait until after the weekend?'

'C-section tomorrow at nine,' he told her. He checked

his watch. 'Providing she holds out tonight. Her blood pressure was up this afternoon and we can't risk waiting longer. She's still trying to run a full-scale office from the ward so we're setting things up for the morning. Tessa, I'm going to head home.'

She hadn't even started adjusting her clothing yet but she looked up at him quickly, her eyes dancing. Once again he was leaving as the time had come for her to feed Thomas. It had become a pattern. At first she'd thought it was the nappies he objected to but when he'd left hurriedly the night before it had suddenly dawned on her that lately he'd been leaving as soon as she even mentioned breastfeeding.

They had specialist lactation nurses at the hospital for mothers who experienced difficulties but it wasn't uncommon for them as doctors to have to examine technique and advise on it so he must have seen hundreds if not thousands of women feeding and she found it funny that with her he was self-conscious.

Experimentally, she started lifting her shirt, and when he turned sharply away from her towards the door she knew for sure she was right. 'You're embarrassed to watch me,' she accused.

'Of course I'm not.' But her instincts told her he wasn't being truthful. 'I'll see you Saturday morning.'

'I'm very discreet.' Remembering the way she'd flashed her breasts at him accidentally after her massage on her first night home, she understood why he might think she wouldn't be, but she tried to reassure him. 'I promise you won't see anything. You really don't have to rush away.' He hadn't even eaten yet. He'd called in straight after work on his way home to bring her some new articles on foetal distress, one of her special-interest subjects. He'd thought she'd be interested in them and she hadn't had the heart to tell him that in her current state of tiredness it had been more than a month since she'd read even a headline in a newspaper. 'Make yourself a sandwich,' she suggested. 'Or there're plenty of biscuits in the cupboard. I'm wearing a maternity bra so I'm perfectly decent. I promise not to shock you.'

'You don't have to tell me there're plenty of biscuits. You made me buy four packets for you yesterday. And I'm not shocked or embarrassed. Goodnight.'

'Goodnight.' She didn't believe his assurances and she felt embarrassed that he was embarrassed and she lowered her head, her nod goodbye distracted. 'See you Saturday.' She knew he was on call the next day for twenty-four hours until Saturday morning. 'Thanks.'

Happily Ellen Wentworth's Caesarean section was straightforward the next morning. Her baby was active and lively although because he was small and premature the paediatrician attending the delivery wanted to watch over him in the hospital's special care baby unit.

Nathan agreed with his anaesthetist's decision to transfer Ellen to Intensive Care for twenty-four hours of monitoring. She'd opted for an epidural so she'd been conscious throughout the operation – with the advantage that epidurals generally lowered blood pressure and avoided the risk of a surge in blood pressure at the beginning of a general anaesthetic – although she'd had some sedation. Not enough to stop her being awake enough on transfer to manage a husky request for her laptop to be brought across to the unit.

Nathan put on his blandest expression. 'Ask me again in a week.'

She wailed weakly but then drifted straight off to sleep.

Ellen's Caesarean was Nathan's only scheduled operation for the morning and he went straight from ICU to clinic. Honour looked relieved when she saw him. 'Mrs Lee's turned up for her appointment and she's due next Wednesday but it sounds as if she's in labour. She's been having contractions for six hours.'

Nathan ran over her clinic observations and latest test results before he moved to the examining room. The mother-to-be looked calm but her husband's hands were white where they gripped hers. One of the clinic's nurses was busy with the machine that monitored uterine contractions and the baby's heart rate.

'Six minutes apart and regular,' she told him.

Nathan nodded. 'Everything's looking fine,' he reassured the couple after checking the tracing. The three contractions captured in the interval they'd recorded so far were strong and orderly, the baby's heart rate had jumped a little in a normal response to each contraction. 'You're definitely in labour.'

Mrs Lee said, 'We weren't sure if we made a mistake coming here instead of telephoning the labour ward.'

'It makes no difference to us. Here's easier for me in fact this morning because I can see you right away.'

At the next contraction, the mother-to-be's expression turned surprised. 'Oh!' she gasped. 'I think the baby's coming!'

They worked fast and it took less than fifteen minutes to deliver a rather startled looking baby who looked bemused by his rapid entry into the world but was, happily, completely healthy.

'He's beautiful,' the paediatric registrar on call assured them, returning the towel-wrapped, wide-eyed baby to his excited father once he'd finished examining him and checking his airways.

Nathan was needed in clinic so he washed and changed and went straight back down, but he called into Mansfield later in the day to see how she was going.

'Oh, very well, doctor.' She was feeding her new baby and she looked up with a tranquil expression.

Nathan smiled at the vigorous sucking movements the infant was making. Even in the first hours after birth the strength of a healthy neonate's survival instincts never failed to amaze him.

Delivery Suite was busy most of the night. In the morning Mrs Lee and her baby were both well and Ellen Wentworth's blood pressure had settled enough for ICU to transfer her earlier than they'd all expected to Mansfield.

Ellen had elected not to breastfeed long-term because of the problems that would create with her work, but she'd decided to try it for the first three weeks before she returned to work full time. Nathan smiled as he came into her side room and saw her sitting in bed, clearly entranced by the baby cradled against her breast.

'What?' he teased. 'No laptop? No secretary? Not even a dictation machine?'

'I'm having a day off,' she declared, looking up with a wry smile. 'I decided I deserve one.'

'You certainly do. The paediatricians were happy with Webster this morning then.'

'He was allowed to come to the ward an hour ago,' she confirmed, nodding. 'He's allowed to stay with me tonight.' The baby released her nipple and Ellen picked him up and turned him to face Nathan. 'Come on, Webster,' she said lightly, bouncing him. 'Say hello to the nasty doctor. He's been horrible to your mummy for weeks.'

'Why, because I vetoed two board-meetings at your bedside?'

'And hid my batteries and phone recharger,' she chided. 'Don't think I don't know who ordered that to disappear last week.'

'It got your blood pressure down.' Nathan grinned. 'Ellen, the poor child's going to vomit on you if you keep jiggling him like that after a feed.'

'Of course he's not…' But she broke off and winced as her baby lived up to Nathan's prediction and promptly dribbled a thread of thin fluid down her hand and arm. 'Ah,' she said gruffly. 'So you know something about these creatures.'

'I've picked up a thing or two.' He pulled a stack of tissues from the packet on her bedside table, passed them to her, then wiped Webster's little face himself when she seemed unsure where to start. 'Poor boy. Mummy has a lot to learn, doesn't she?'

'That's right.' Ellen wiped her arm. 'First thing Mummy's going to learn is to pass you to the nanny quick smart in future,' she murmured. But her gaze as she surveyed her son was loving and Nathan wondered if she was going to find it as easy to give up the day-to-day care of her son as she'd planned before his birth. 'So how long are you going to keep me in prison?'

'Until you're ready to leave,' he said mildly. 'Keep wearing your stockings and stretch your toes and flex your calves at least fifteen times an hour.'

He checked her charts and briefly examined her heart and chest and tummy and told her he'd be in to review things Monday morning.

He pulled up on the street below Tessa's home a few minutes before ten. She'd obviously been watching for him because when he got to the first switchback she'd started down from the top, clutching pages of newspaper adverts, her phone in her hand. 'He's fast asleep,' she told him breathlessly when they met several levels higher. 'I'm seeing the first place in ten minutes.' She reached up and kissed him and instead of her usual delicate floral fragrance he found himself briefly enveloped in the scent of Thomas' baby powder. 'Thanks so much for this, Nathan. There're ten places I want to see. Call me if Thomas wakes and I'll come back early.'

'Take these.' It was sultry with only the lightest of breezes, and temperatures were predicted to soar above thirty. Her pink cheeks warned him she was already feeling the heat and he offered her the keys to his car. It would be vastly more comfortable than hers. 'The air conditioning will help keep you cool.'

'What if I dent it?'

'You can pay my excess.'

Her dimples appeared and she took the keys. 'I suppose it'll impress prospective landlords. Thomas might not seem such a disadvantage if they think I'm rich. Perhaps I should have dressed up?'

'You look fine.' More than fine. In the sunny, loosely-cut sleeveless jerkin and long, floaty summer skirt and straw hat she wore she looked youthful and breezy and radiant and he felt suddenly light-hearted himself. 'Have fun.'

'See you soon.' She waved as she went down the next flight of steps. 'Be sure to call if he needs me.'

Nathan checked Thomas when he got up to the house but he was still sleeping. He was on his back – since the finding that that position reduced the risk of sudden infant death, a baby in any other position seemed unnatural to him – with a light, cotton blanket tucked around him. Nathan studied him for a few pensive moments then headed out into the living room.

He kept checking him and when Thomas woke after a couple of hours and called out a small protest Nathan examined him and changed his nappy thinking that was the problem. He held him, clucking at him to reassure him, and took him for a walk around the house but although the baby looked at him bemusedly and fell silent for a few minutes, he soon started grizzling again. The way he suckled enthusiastically at the knuckle of Nathan's little finger told him Thomas needed something he couldn't give him.

'You want your mum do you, pal?' Nathan rocked him gently and grinned down at his little face as he carried him out towards Tessa's telephone. 'I bet you do,' he murmured. 'I bet she's all you can think about right now. Well trust me, Tom, I know exactly what you're going through. Lately I've been finding it hard to think of anything but your gorgeous mother myself. Let's go call her, shall we?'

Tessa arrived at the front door before he finished punching in her number. She looked up and smiled at him with Thomas but Nathan noted her breathlessness and the dispirited, almost weary light in her eyes and frowned.

'What are you saying to my son?' she demanded, coming over to them, her arms outstretched, some of the weariness evaporating as she laughed at Thomas. 'What are you whispering about, hmm? Are you corrupting my Thomas, Nathan?'

'We're talking man stuff,' he said dryly. 'Not good?'

'I'm sure it'll improve before I'm thrown out on the streets but today was about as bad as it could be.' Thomas had stopped complaining the instant Tessa had taken over and now he lifted his little hands and tangled her hair in his fingers. 'This time over summer's not a good time to be looking apparently. I saw a few absolute dumps that will take children and some nice places that won't, and the one that might have done was at a corner and really noisy with cars revving all the time. Maybe I'm being too fussy, but I've got Thomas to think about now. I want him to live somewhere nice. Hello, my darling.'

'I've changed him but he's hungry.'

'I'll feed him. I need to anyway, I'm sore as anything.' She backed towards the couch. 'I see you've heard your cue,' she remarked calmly when he started to turn away. 'I was planning to make lunch for you but I see you're going to flee in horror instead.'

Nathan sighed. 'You're wrong.'

'I don't think so.' She swivelled Thomas around onto her lap.

'You must be thirsty after being outside.' He kept his eyes firmly on her face as she unbuttoned her jerkin. 'Tea or juice?'

'Tea please.' He felt her eyes on his back as he turned away towards the kitchen counter. 'You prude, you're not fooling me. Your car drives like a dream by the way.'

'So keep it.'

'*What?*'

'Keep it.' He'd thought about it while she'd been gone. 'I'm not using it for much except going to and from work at the moment. We'll swap for a month or so while the weather's so warm. There're fittings to install Thomas' capsule in the back and the air conditioning will keep him cool if we get another long spell of heat like this.'

'That's crazy.'

Nathan glanced up from where he was preparing the tea then relaxed a little as he saw that the way she'd arranged herself and Thomas meant her breasts were concealed.

'You can't give me your car,' she added incredulously.

'I didn't mean give, I meant lend. Temporarily. It's a sensible idea.'

'It's not sensible,' she argued, 'it's ridiculous. I appreciate you offering, and thank you but no.'

'Look, Tessa...'

'Don't you *patronise* me.' She sounded cheerful enough but her mouth and chin had taken on the determined shapes he recognised as Tessa at her most mulish. 'And don't you narrow your eyes at me like that, because you of all people should know by now that I'm immune to your sexy charms.'

'You're being unreasonably stubborn.' He studied her impatiently. 'It's a good idea.'

'One I can manage without.' She stared back at him. 'I thank you and I love you for your thoughtfulness, but no, Nathan. My little car is fine.'

'We'll talk about this later,' he warned, coming towards her with her tea.

'In your dreams.' She lifted Thomas and swapped him to her other side and Nathan, caught by surprise by the movement and the inadvertent and sudden exposure of creamy curved flesh and a tight, puckered nipple, froze. 'Really, forget it. You need your car...'

But she broke off and he caught her accusing expression and realised she'd seen his shock. 'It *is* my breasts,' she exclaimed, drawing her shirt closed. 'I can't believe it. You're really embarrassed!'

Nathan drew back sharply. 'Of course I'm not.'

'Liar. Look at your face.'

Nathan refrained from asking how, exactly, without a mirror, he was supposed to do that. He walked away from her and collected his keys from the counter where she'd dropped them before taking Thomas. 'I'm not embarrassed,' he repeated. Although he might be if he stayed. 'I'll see you next week…'

'Don't be silly. You don't have to rush away. Stay for lunch. You're a doctor. Even if you weren't, I wouldn't care. A mother feeding her baby is the most natural thing in the world.'

He gritted his teeth. 'I know that.'

'Then why can't you bear to see me do it?'

'Because at the moment I can't close my eyes and not picture you rubbing olive oil into yourself,' he said harshly, her ridiculous lack of awareness taunting him to a purely frustrated response. 'Considering that image has kept me awake at nights for the best part of a week already I don't need the added stimulation of seeing you feed Thomas and imagining myself in his place. Is that clear enough for you, Tessa, or shall I draw you a picture?'

chapter seven

Tessa went into the hospital on Tuesday. She had files to collect from her office and she wanted to borrow a few journals from the library. As little as she still felt like working it worried her that her brain might turn to mush if she didn't at least make some effort. Besides, she'd promised the nurses on the wards that she'd bring Thomas to visit as soon as she felt energetic enough to manage it.

The staff on Mansfield gathered round and raved about him. 'He's so cute,' Rita, the nurse manager proclaimed. 'He's got your chin, Tessa.'

'So everyone keeps telling me.' Tessa wondered what exactly it was about her chin that was so distinctive. Since Thomas' birth she'd spent a lot of time studying it in the mirror but to her, her chin still looked much the same as everyone else's. Her gaze drifted to the white-board listing the names of the ward's patients beside the nursing station. 'Oh, Ellen's still here.'

'Until tomorrow,' Rita told her. 'Nathan told her she can go home after Mr Austin's round.'

Tessa called in to see her. Originally she'd been supervising Ellen's antenatal care but Nathan, because he'd taken over her clinical load when she'd had to give up work the day before she'd had Thomas, was looking after her now.

The other woman looked delighted to see her. To Tessa's surprise she was alone in her room with her baby rather than surrounded by co-workers and her laptop lay dormant and closed up on a shelf on her bedside table.

'Hey,' Tessa chided after their greetings and baby introductions, 'what's happened to the workaholic?'

'The workaholic had a baby,' Ellen told her ruefully, shifting Webster slightly in her arms. 'I've discovered he's more demanding than a full-time job.'

'I know what you mean.' Tessa smiled sympathetically. 'Are you still hoping to get straight back into work when you leave here?'

'Perhaps only part-time to start,' the other woman conceded. 'And I've decided to have two months at home first. I didn't realise how much this would take out of me. What about you?'

'I'm hoping to get back in another three weeks,' Tessa told her. The longer she was away from work the more she thought she'd like longer but she had little choice. 'I need the money and if my career isn't to suffer long term I have to keep pulling my weight,' she explained. 'Besides, it's not fair on my colleagues if I delay my time away because they couldn't get funding for a locum to cover me so they're all working longer hours.'

'Nathan's been great,' Ellen reassured her. 'He does seem to be here all the time though.'

'He's incredibly dedicated,' Tessa agreed. 'I've learned a lot from him.'

'He's sexy as hell,' Ellen said lightly, with a grin. 'I love those capable, commanding types. I notice he doesn't wear a ring.'

'I think he's seeing a doctor who works in the city.' Tessa lowered her eyes. It frightened her a little that that continued to niggle at her. 'Nathan and Georgette went out for a while a year ago,' she added, her tone determinedly cheerful. 'He refuses to talk about her but I have a feeling he's still very keen.'

'Lucky girl,' Ellen said dryly.

'I only hope she realises it.' Tessa looked down at Thomas, her brow creasing. She hadn't seen Nathan since Saturday when he'd made those peculiar comments about olive oil and her breasts then walked out on her, slamming the door so hard her house had shaken.

She knew him well enough to know that those remarks had been seriously out of character.

What she absolutely didn't believe was that he found her attractive sexually. Not Nathan. That was beyond credence. Not after all this time and not when he of all people understood *all* her inadequacies and weaknesses and certainly not with her looking all blown up and battle-weary the way she looked these days.

What made more sense was that he still felt so bad about his role in matchmaking her with Simon that her comments about never becoming involved with a man again had made him feel compelled to take on the job of reassuring her that one might one day find her attractive again.

The thought of him feeling sorry for her made her squirm. It might be a thoughtful, generous, unselfish thing he was trying to do to – and that was entirely *in* character – and she loved him for it but still she couldn't stand it. It was too embarrassing.

In the meantime, while he was spending so much time with her he had to be neglecting his real love life. It occurred to her suddenly that since Georgette was probably unhappy about that – she might even be jealous – then it might help if she called her and explained the whole Simon thing and exactly why it was that Nathan felt so obliged to help them.

Nathan appeared in her kitchen the next evening when

she was stir-frying vegetables and sliced chicken. She'd left her bottom door open and he simply walked upstairs without knocking and glared at her. 'What,' he demanded, 'have you been saying?'

Tessa turned down the heat under her wok and blinked at him. It bemused her that he could get up all her steps without puffing. As far as she knew he didn't work out. Unlike Simon who used to spend hours every week working out in front of the mirrors at the most fashionable gym in town, she didn't think Nathan even belonged to one. Yet he ran up stairs at the hospital with so little effort he could as easily have been standing on an escalator and he kept appearing in her home breathing calmly. Natural fitness, she thought vaguely. He must be one of those rare people who were always naturally fit. 'I haven't done anything.'

'Liar.' Annoyed green eyes narrowed at her. 'Last night there was a message on my machine from Georgette. Today when I get out of Theatres there's another one on my bleep with more on the wards. When I finally get a chance to call her now I get some babble about you insisting I'm pining away for her.'

'Ah.' Tessa brushed her food away from the hot centre of the wok with a wooden spoon then turned off the heat completely. 'Ah, yes.'

'Try again.' Nathan folded his arms, his face hard and she blinked again, a little worried. She wasn't used to him looking hard. 'What are you up to?'

'Trying to help. Trying to do you a favour if you must know. You're spending too much of your free time with me and not enough with Georgette. You obviously know it because you keep telling me you're not going to be able to come for a week or so but then you turn up anyway.

Clearly you have this bizarre feeling of obligation to us still but I've already told you that that's silly. It's time you straightened things out with Georgette. You should be thanking me for calling when I did. She had no idea you were still besotted. She thought your relationship, such as it was, was over ages ago.'

'She thinks that because it's true.'

'Only because you haven't told her how you feel,' she argued. 'What is it with you? Why can't you see that I'm happy? I don't need you the way you think. I'm fine on my own. Truly. I'm managing. Concentrate on your own life. Surely you're not still clinging to the idea that you can't marry for another year or more. Or is that you're so used to being in control of everything and anything that the thought of admitting you love a woman enough to make you maybe reconsider that plan is simply terrifying for you?'

'You had no right to interfere…'

'If you don't do something now you'll lose her,' she warned. 'She's been seeing someone. I could tell from her voice that she likes you more but you'll have to move fast.'

'You have no idea.'

'I know enough to know you needed to be pushed. If you want me to apologise for interfering, I will, of course I will, but inside I still feel I did the right thing. You're my friend and you've done a lot for me. I wanted to help you back. Have you asked her out?'

But he sighed and looked at her as if he she'd grown a second head. 'Why would I do that?'

She shook her head, not understanding. 'You're being silly,' she insisted. 'You'll lose her if you keep playing games. You have to tell her how you feel.'

'I've told her exactly.'

Tessa's heart thudded. She blinked. 'Oh.' She turned her head and thought about that and felt angry that it didn't make her feel as good as it should have. 'Well, that has to be good.'

'Whatever.' Nathan lifted one shoulder as if the outcome was unimportant. 'I've decided that you and Thomas are coming to live at the house.'

Tessa drew her brows together then shook her head slightly again and decided she'd definitely misunderstood this time. 'Oh, that's great news. You've asked Georgette to move in with you at last, have you?'

'Not Georgette.' His narrowed look suggested he thought her mad. 'You and Thomas. You and Thomas are coming to live with me.'

'No we're not.'

He folded his arms. 'I'm not going to argue with you on this.'

'I wouldn't care if you argued till you were blue in the face,' she retorted. 'It wouldn't make any difference.'

'In ten days you're going to be evicted,' he reminded her, unnecessarily since the thought was never out of her head. 'You have a baby son, nowhere to stay, no immediate prospect of finding anywhere judging by the luck you've had so far, you have no income so you've probably not enough spare money to pay for a motel for anything more than a few nights and you have no family to help. I, on the other hand, have four empty bedrooms, two bathrooms I have never used, loads of space and a sudden craving for company.'

'I refuse to impose…'

'Since you've never been able to take with one hand without giving with two, if your conscience is the problem, then pay me rent. Or better still, you can draw up ideas for a native garden for me. I want flax bushes, cabbage trees, a bunch of grasses, maybe a toi-toi or two and some hebes, you know the sort of thing. You know plants and I haven't had time to even think about them.'

Tessa closed her mouth, thought a little, then opened it again. 'I'm happy to do that for you, of course I am, but I've looked at some quite nice motels over the last two days. They're not that expensive, especially once you get out of the city, if you stay long enough.'

'You're not taking Thomas to a motel,' he said stonily.

'In the short term it won't do either of us any harm.'

'Neither will I.' He spoke as if it was a done deal. 'There's another condition. I don't want you contacting Georgette again.'

Tessa tilted up her chin. Not being able to talk to Georgette wasn't an issue, she knew. In fact it was irrelevant. Now that the other woman had a little more insight into Nathan's feelings it was up to her to take things further. 'There's one motel that's really very, very nice. The units have lovely kitchens and there's plenty of room…'

'You're coming to the house. Either on your own two feet or kicking and screaming across my shoulder. I will not let you stay in a motel and I will not let you take Thomas to one. Stop being so stubborn. For once in your life admit that someone else might be right.'

'This is not your decision.' She felt helpless. She hadn't been looking forward to moving into a motel and the idea of staying with Nathan, of having a small breathing space at least meaning she wouldn't have to rush into a lease on an unsuitable flat, was unbearably tempting. But how in the world would she ever be able to pay him back? 'I want to be independent.'

He'd walked to the main window and now he stared out, his back to her. 'I'll ring Simon then, shall I? We'll ask him what he thinks about you bringing up his son in a motel when there's a perfectly good alternative available.'

'You wouldn't,' she gasped.

'Try me.' He turned around and surveyed her stunned expression impassively. 'He's still in Thailand, isn't he?'

'I don't know. I suppose so.' She was breathless. 'You'd really go behind my back like that?'

'I'll be doing it to your face. You can talk to him if you want.'

'No!' Not unless Simon wanted her to. There was so much about Thomas that she ached to share with him. But she couldn't call him because he wouldn't see it as a sign of her simply wanting to tell him about their son or of her being concerned for him and wanting to be sure that he was all right and had everything he needed. He'd see it as her harassing him. She reached out blindly behind her and grabbed the arm of a chair and sank slowly into it. 'I can't believe you'd do that to me.'

'I don't want to hurt you and I'm not trying to bully you.' His hands had curled into fists, she saw, but when he saw her looking at them he shoved them into the pockets of his pants. 'Well, maybe I am trying to bully you a little. But only because I want you to see sense. I can't stand by and see you take Thomas to a motel.'

'It's not that I don't want to come…'

'Then stop arguing with me and say thank you.'

She stared at him for a few seconds, then finally, admitting defeat, said, 'Thank you.' She felt dazed. 'All right. You're very kind. But I also have to make a condition of my own.'

'Go on.'

'The other night you said something about thinking about me with the olive oil.'

'I remember.'

'Well,' she lifted her eyes and forced her gaze to stay steady, 'I wanted to say that I don't want you to pretend with me, Nathan. I understand why you said all that and I appreciate it, I do appreciate your thoughtfulness, but it doesn't help me. To be honest, it mixes me up. I'd prefer you didn't say anything else like that again.'

There was silence for a few seconds then he said quietly, 'How about we start with you explaining "pretend"?'

She was puzzled that he wanted her to go that far, but at least, she recognised, that way there would be no misunderstandings. He would understand that she knew everything. 'You think Simon leaving the way he did means I'm an emotional wreck,' she stated bluntly. 'You're worried about me so you're on a mission to convince me I'm not physically repugnant.'

There was a brief silence at that and then, 'And are you an emotional wreck?'

'Dented more than wrecked I'd have said.' And she was over the worst of it. 'I've a few bumps and bruises, but I'm not about to throw myself off a bridge if that's what you're worried about.'

'Were you ever?'

'No.' She looked back at him steadily. 'Not over Simon. In the past, once or twice, in my darkest moments after the accident I remember the thought sliding into my head once or twice. But I was nineteen and I was lonely and even then it never went any further than a thought. It wouldn't even get that far now. Certainly not because of a man. If I've learned anything it's that men aren't worth that much. The pain always goes away in the end and there comes a time a while later when you can hardly remember them. Besides, I have Thomas now. I have a lot to live for.'

Nathan studied her almost broodingly for a few more seconds, then said, 'I'll call a removal firm in the morning and book for Saturday. There's no reason to see out the end of your lease here and if you give me the landlady's number I'll organise that extra month's rent refund she promised you.'

'I'll do that myself.' Tessa didn't mind that he hadn't acknowledged the sense of everything she'd said, she told herself, because her point had been made. 'Saturday's too soon.' The heavy furniture and appliances belonged with the house but she still had a lot of belongings, including bookcases full of medical books and journals, Simon's, as well as her own. 'It'll take me till next week at least to pack.'

'Removal people pack. That's what you pay them for. They'll bring boxes and wrapping and all you have to do is look after Thomas. Good. I'm glad you're seeing sense.' He looked around, apparently satisfied although to Tessa's way of thinking he should look more fearful than content. It worried her that he was under-anticipating the extra fuss having her and Thomas in his household, however temporarily, was going to create. 'That smells interesting.'

Collecting her thoughts she stood and walked across to her wok. 'It's chicken stir-fry. I made enough for you in case you came.'

'I'd like some, thanks.' Now he'd got his own way he seemed almost back to his usual relaxed self, and his shrug was a typically casual Nathan one and Tessa felt herself beginning to relax again. 'I missed lunch and I'm starving.'

It was another of what had been a long string of warm nights and she served the meal outside on the cane outdoor setting that belonged to the house. For dessert Tessa had one of the chocolate yoghurts she'd bought that day but Nathan turned up his nose when she offered him one and chose fruit instead.

'It's not yoghurt,' he taunted when she defended her sweet from his scathing look. 'It says "dairy dessert".'

'Which means a sort of yoghurt,' she argued. 'It's still healthy.'

'Hardly.' He spooned the last scoop of his kiwi fruit into his mouth and ate it then eased himself out of his chair and collected their plates. 'I'm going. I need to do some reading tonight. Stay there,' he added, when she went to stand. 'Relax for five minutes for once. I'll check Thomas on my way through. I'll be in touch tomorrow.'

Privately Tessa thought Nathan had been exaggerating the talents of the removal firm but the two uniformed men who arrived at her door early Saturday morning equipped with clip-boards and packing materials were awe-inspiringly efficient and they had every one of her possessions carefully packed into cartons before lunch. By three she was sitting on the edge of Nathan's swimming pool under the shade of the sail cloth he'd had installed, happily dangling her feet in the water while she read to Thomas and gave him his afternoon feed, still dazed by the whirl-wind speed of her transfer to their new home.

'*Temporary* home,' she reminded Thomas. 'So don't get too used to living in luxury, Thomas Mitchell

Morrison. You're only going to be here a week or two until I find us a flat.' But while she was here, for the short time they lived in Nathan's home, she was determined to do everything she could to make Nathan's life easier.

He arrived home just after she got back to the pool after putting Thomas down in his cot in his new room. The fence around the pool was clear between the railings and she saw him park his car and waved and he lifted his hand in acknowledgement as he climbed out.

'Sorry I couldn't get home early enough to help,' he called, when he came closer. 'It was a busy night then I had to go to theatre this morning.'

'It was fine.' She put aside the pad she'd brought out to begin her landscaping plans and smiled at him. She'd known he was on call the night before and although he'd told her he'd come to the house to help out after his morning ward round she hadn't been surprised when he hadn't made it. Obstetrics was an unpredictable speciality and working hours were never fixed. 'The removal men were great,' she assured him. 'I hardly did a thing.'

'All settled then?'

'I have to go back in the morning and finish cleaning. I want to wash out the kitchen cupboards now they're empty and the windows need doing as well, but apart from that, yes. What was the emergency?' Many of the women who'd be coming in to give birth over the next few weeks were ones she'd followed antenatally. 'Any one I know?'

'Primary haemorrhage from a retained placenta. And you don't know her, no, but she's going to be fine. Enjoying the sun?'

'The shade at least,' she agreed, gazing up at the sail. 'Isn't it a lovely day?'

'Too lovely for Wellington. This summer must be getting into the record books. There's hardly been a decent gale in weeks.' He put the papers he was carrying under his arm and headed for the door. 'Where have you put yourself?'

'In the big room at the end,' she called out. 'The one furthest from yours so we won't disturb you at night. Thomas is in the blue one beside me. Is that all right?'

'Fine. Anywhere.' He lifted his spare hand in acknowledgement but didn't look back as he walked into the house.

Tessa tucked her dress up around the middle of her thighs and lazed back beneath the sail, her feet still in the water, letting her eyes close, electing to try mentally landscaping his section before she started drawing. Nathan came out a little while later. She heard his feet on the tiles and then the sound of him diving cleanly into the pool and beginning to swim but she was too lazy to sit up. She opened her eyes only when the splashing stopped a long time later and she heard him lifting himself out of the water.

'That was very energetic,' she said sleepily when he came to sit next to her. 'It also explains why you're so fit. I thought you didn't do anything.'

'Not as much as I should.' She saw his arm lift above her and tiny droplets of water fell from his fingers to splatter teasingly across her face, making her screw it up in protest. 'Sleepyhead,' he accused. 'Why don't you get on a lounger so you can rest in comfort? I'll keep an eye on Thomas for a few hours.'

'I'm not sleepy, just lazy.' To prove it she sat up. She looked at him properly then swallowed heavily.

It was a while since she'd last seen Nathan in

swimmers and she'd forgotten how spectacular he was. His green shorts were modest compared with the tight Speedos Simon preferred, but still she was aware of feeling a little flustered. Outside of a background awareness of Nathan's attractiveness, she'd never thought much about his body. Now she had a feeling she might find it hard to think about anything else. His shoulders and chest and stomach were smooth and hard looking and the sheen left by the water highlighted the powerful muscles beneath the skin. His thighs next to hers were perfectly in proportion with the rest of his body but made hers look thin and almost fragile in comparison. The differences in the two men hadn't been that obvious beneath their clothes – Simon was probably as tall as Nathan and he took his work outs seriously – but once the clothes were off Simon would look almost slight next to his friend.

'No wonder Georgette sounded so thrilled when I rang her,' she breathed. 'If obstetrics ever gets boring you could always make a living as a model.'

'Ha ha.' He captured the experimental finger she put out to test the texture of his chest and curled his hand around it. 'Don't start anything you don't mean to finish,' he warned lightly.

'Oh yes?' Tessa wrinkled her nose, wondering if his teasing counted as a sort of fake compliment, but it didn't seem worth the fuss to bother with it and so she let it go and smiled and took her finger back. 'We've talked about this.'

'I remember.' His eyes narrowed down. 'You think I'm pretending.'

'I know you are.' She smiled a satisfied smile and subsided back on to the warm paving beneath the sail, her feet still in the water. She wasn't able to swim yet – it was too soon after Thomas' birth and although the chance of picking up an infection from the water had to be remote, she preferred not to take the risk for another two weeks – but she envied Nathan the wet drops clinging to his skin and looked forward to the day she'd finally get to immerse her body in the inviting, blue water. 'But much as I love you for it, I don't need it. It's time you accepted that I'm perfectly happy with my situation and I don't need to be reassured with compliments, however well intentioned.'

'I warned you about making assumptions.' He squeezed her finger lightly before releasing her. 'How can you be sure I haven't lured you here under false pretences to lull you into a false sense of security and have my way with you?'

'Lull away.' Shielding her eyes from the sun with her hand, she beamed up at him. 'Nathan, the way you look in those swimmers, I'd let you have your way with me any time.'

He put on his sunglasses. 'And you feel fairly safe making that offer?'

'Pretty much one hundred per cent safe,' she agreed contentedly. 'Pretty much never safer or surer of anything in my entire life.'

'I can see I've become far too predictable.'

'Mmm.' She lifted her knees and braced her feet against the warm paving. 'It's your finest feature.'

The shock of cold water being dumped over her warm face and throat brought her up spluttering and gasping. 'Oh!'

'Never take anything for granted.' Nathan, fending off her offended looks and batting hands with an arm and an easy grin, scooped up another handful of water and let it drizzle over her bare legs. 'Don't go getting too relaxed because that's when I'll pounce.'

'Sure you will. And being called predictable is a compliment!' Tessa used the sleeve of her T-shirt to wipe her face dry. 'It means you're reliable. But OK, you've made your point. You're wildly unreliable and unstable.'

'Good girl.' He tapped her nose lightly. 'What's this scar?' He shifted his hand and slid it beneath her right leg to cup the underside of her knee and she felt a small, strange curling in the bottom of her stomach. Too much sun, she thought. 'I didn't know you'd had surgery.'

'I stuffed up my medial ligament playing netball at Med School.' She wiped her face again to get rid of the last of the dripping water and propped herself up on her elbows, holding her breath while his fingers probed the pink line.

He looked up at her. 'Want me to kiss it better?'

'I already agreed you're unstable.'

'You didn't sound convinced.'

She laughed as she lay back down. 'Don't fret, you don't have to go that far.'

There was a short, potent silence and then Nathan said lightly. 'Have I ever told you that I've always admired you for being able to pick up your life and choosing to move on? You survived a trauma of the sort most of us only hear about in news stories. That can't have been easy. I remember watching you on the yacht that last afternoon the time we were in the Sounds for the weekend for Simon's birthday. You were petrified.'

She shivered. 'I could tell the wind was coming up,' she remembered. 'And the swell was increasing. It's still hard to trust nature sometimes.' The chartered yacht and the weekend sailing amongst the Marlborough Sounds with a group of friends had been her surprise twenty-eighth birthday present to Simon. He loved sailing and good food and wine and company and the trip had combined them all.

'After the accident with my parents I was in the water for nine hours before the search plane spotted me,' she went on hollowly. 'I found out later that the predicted survival time in that water was only around four but somehow I lasted. The boat capsized too quickly to get the life rafts off but luckily or unluckily I'd found some wreckage to hold on to. It was another three days before they found mum and dad and Trudy.' She closed her eyes briefly. 'I'm not phobic, I grew up around boats and I can still handle them, I was perfectly happy about that weekend. But I...I get nervous when conditions start deteriorating and Simon was having too much fun to want to take the boat back early. Thanks for what you did then.'

Nathan, pleading an urgent case of sea-sickness, had persuaded Simon to let them take the yacht into a quiet cove and they'd anchored in calm waters and Tessa had been able to get off the boat and on to the beach until it was time to head back into Picton. 'I remember thinking at the time that it was strange that you'd never been sick before and you didn't look even slightly green. It didn't occur to me till now that you must have lied about that for me.'

But he shrugged. 'It was more interesting in the bay. The snorkelling was good.' He reached out and touched her hair. 'I wish I'd known you in those first years in Dunedin.'

'Why?' She rolled her eyes. 'So you could have *had your wicked way with me*?'

'No.' He smiled. 'Idiot. So I could have wrapped you up in cotton wool and protected you from yourself until you got better.'

'I'm glad you weren't there.' She yawned again. 'Because then I wouldn't have you now. Mmm, this sun is lovely.' She lay back again. 'My legs are feeling a bit warm. Any chance of getting some sun cream on them?'

'You're pushing it.' But eventually she felt drops of cream fall on to her left leg. 'It's total block,' he murmured. 'It's water resistant so you can put your feet back in the pool if you want.'

'Thanks.' She kept her eyes closed, enjoying the firm and impersonal professional-style strokes of his hands. She'd gathered her skirt up higher so he could do her thighs, then he worked down to her calves and feet. 'I know I'm repeating myself, but you are extraordinarily good at this.'

'Arms.'

Obediently, she passed him her left one to start. Her cotton T-shirt was over-sized and loose and he rubbed cream from the edge of the sleeve right down around her elbow and over her forearm to the tips of her fingers.

When he finished with the left she drooped her right arm across her body to make it easier for him, her eyes still closed. 'Forget modelling,' she said languidly. 'You don't need it. You'd make a fortune as a masseur. Put me down for a back rub too please, if you find the time this week.'

'What about your face?'

Tessa dragged her eyes open and squinted at the tube he held. 'Better not.' She hadn't used that brand of cream before and the skin on her face had been sensitive since her pregnancy.

'Put this over it then.' He covered her face with a broad-rimmed straw hat.

'No doubt a vast improvement,' she pronounced. Her voice came out muffled by the hat. 'Hey, my legs feel like they're still burning,' she chirped, bolder now as she kicked out her feet. 'You can't have put enough cream on. I think you'd better do them again.'

'I think you might be a fraud, Tessa Webster.' But he sounded amused instead of impatient and rather than ignoring her teasing as she'd been sure he would she felt more cream dribble on to her warm left thigh. 'Sybarite.'

'I think you might be turning me into one.' She closed her eyes blissfully as his hands began spreading the cream. 'Mmm. That feels divine. You're spoiling me.'

'It's about time someone did.'

Her eyes flickered open. She tipped back the hat and their gazes met. Hers, she knew, would be a little startled but his return regard was enigmatic behind his sunglasses and, vaguely reassured, she replaced the hat and let her eyes close again.

Astonishingly, she must have drifted off to sleep because when a noise roused her again Nathan was standing next to her, dressed in shorts and a loose blue shirt, and he was holding Thomas.

'How'd I get here?' Tessa sat up and suddenly realised that instead of being by the pool she was lying on one of the loungers. 'Did you carry me? Your poor back. What time is it?'

'Almost six.' He lifted one broad shoulder and handed a wailing Thomas over to her when she put out her arms. 'Your feet were wrinkled from the water and I thought you'd be more comfortable here and my back is fine, thank you. You're a feather-weight.'

'Hardly.' Tessa was shocked she could have been oblivious for so long. 'Six!' she exclaimed. 'Poor Thomas.' She kissed his tummy and blew a raspberry on it then cuddled him and soothed and jiggled and clucked at him until he stopped complaining. 'Poor, poor Thomas. Has your mummy been neglecting you? You must be so hungry, my darling.' Automatically she checked his nappy but he was wearing a fresh one. 'And thanks for changing him.' She sobered. 'I am sorry.'

'For what?' There was a tinge of impatience in the green regard that slid across her then. 'I'm glad you could sleep. I wouldn't have woken you if Thomas hadn't demanded I did.' Nathan half-turned back to the house. 'You must be thirsty. Juice or tea?'

'Juice please.' She smiled her thanks in a distracted way as she started lifting her T-shirt. 'Half and half with water so it's not too strong. Thanks.'

Tessa had intended cooking a roast for dinner but her nap had left her languid more than refreshed and she knew the leg of lamb she'd bought would take almost two hours to prepare, so she agreed immediately when Nathan suggested takeaway pizza. 'As long as I pay,' she insisted.

He granted her a weary look but he did, to her relief, take the notes she offered him. While he was out she took a hurried shower to scrub off the sun-cream. A light wind had sprung up, lowering the air temperature, and she changed into one of the loose cotton dresses that had happily seen her through all but the last month of her pregnancy and added a lightweight cardigan over top.

'This is like paradise,' she announced with a smile, looking up from where she'd been sorting through the music collection stacked in a rack in one corner of his open-plan living area when Nathan arrived back with the food. 'I feel as if I'm staying in a fabulous hotel. I've got a pool and entertainment and sun cream and massages on demand. And look at this view!' She rose and lifted her arms towards the broad timber-framed glass framing the bush and harbour and city vista before them. 'You realise, of course, that you're stuck with Thomas and me for life now.'

Her gentle taunting was deliberate since she was sure the prospect would horrify him, but he merely shrugged. 'I've had worse houseguests. When Jack was down on his last holiday one of the girlfriends he had back to stay brought a dog that ate the stuffing out of my chairs. Do you want to eat in here?'

'Yes please.' She smiled again, remembering that Nathan's mother had mentioned his brother enjoyed playing the field. 'He's a bit of a playboy, Jack, is he?'

'A *bit*?' Nathan grimaced. 'Major understatement.'

Tessa smiled again at the reproof in his voice. If she hadn't known otherwise she'd have assumed then that Nathan was the elder of the two. 'You know you could be the same, if you wanted, Nathan. You've got the looks and you've definitely got the body.'

'Drop it, Tessa.' He wasn't smiling and so she let it pass.

'What's in the bags?'

'Salad and a treat for you.' He put the pizza boxes down on to the coffee table. 'Another juice or would you prefer wine or a beer?'

'Water's fine.' She hadn't been able to drink orange juice at all during her pregnancy and overdosing on it now still tended to give her indigestion. While he was collecting plates and their drinks she chose music and put it into his sound system. They ate at the table. The pizzas were thin-crusted the way she liked them, hot and dripping with topping, and she made a mess and managed to get oil and tomato all over her face and hands. Nathan, his expression mingled exasperation and tolerance, used the paper napkins that had come with the food to wipe her mouth and cheeks. 'Infant,' he chided, when she poked out her tongue at him in response to his tutting. 'How are you going to teach Thomas good manners when you're worse than any toddler?'

'I'm not as bad as Thomas,' she protested, with a laugh. She reached for the single-serve chocolate cheesecake that had been his surprise for her. 'I, at least, promise to never vomit on your pillow.'

'Throw up anywhere you like. It's important you feel at home.' But he looked doubtful as he watched her peeling back the top of the dessert. 'My pillow? Really?'

'Sorry.' Tessa licked the cream-coated foil lid of the dessert. 'Thomas started crying when we first got here and I needed somewhere private away from the movers to feed him. Your bedroom was the only one they weren't putting stuff in and your bed looked so big and warm and comfortable that I couldn't resist putting my feet up for a few minutes, only afterwards he had a tiny spill.'

'OK.'

But she knew it wasn't. 'I washed the case and the pillow straight away and I've put a fresh one on the bed for you,' she assured him, between mouthfuls of the cheesecake. 'You'll never know, I promise. And it won't happen again. From now on I'll make your room a no-go area for both of us.'

'I don't mind.' Apparently recovered from the shock, he shrugged. 'Feel free to come into my bedroom whenever you want.'

'Said spider to the fly.' She smiled. 'Coming from anyone else, that'd almost sound like a proposition.' But when he didn't say anything, when he just smiled blandly, she laughed. 'Don't worry. I was teasing. I'm not going to jump on you in the night. It means the world to me that we can be friends without ever worrying about sex. I wouldn't change that for anything.'

chapter eight

Despite her best intentions, two weeks into their stay at Nathan's and only a few days before she'd originally planned to go back to work, Tessa wasn't any closer to finding somewhere permanent to live. What she wanted was a two-bedroomed house, within the city or close to the hospital, preferably one with some character, with a fenced garden with room for Thomas to play in once he was older, in a quiet setting, with a long lease. What she was being shown were big, run-down, draughty or damp houses with sections opening directly on to busy roads with leases short enough to make it likely that the owners might be planning to sell when the market was right.

She was growing cynical about newspaper advertisements and real estate agents. 'Convenient', she'd discovered, meant a house was on a main road. 'Character' meant parts of it were falling down. She wouldn't have minded one of those too much if she was still on her own but Thomas, she felt, deserved better. 'Views', 'quiet' and 'big garden' were dreams and out of her budget.

She had more luck the next week and by Saturday she'd drawn up a list of possible places so that Nathan – who insisted on checking everything over before she committed herself – could inspect them with her on his first day off. He labelled the first house a dump. He said he could tell from the street that it was structurally unsound and probably about to fall off the hill with the next decent wind and he wouldn't even get out of the car to look at it. The second house looked nice from the outside. It was quiet and the section was well fenced and once she did a bit of weeding and mowed the lawns it would have a pretty garden, but Nathan's review of this one too was scathing. The sub-floor drainage was poor, he told her. It was damp and the foundations were suspect. And it faced south and the north and west windows were shaded by trees so it wouldn't get any sun in winter. And the house over the back fence was for sale and since the section was large he imagined developers would sub-divide it so there'd be building noise all day for months.

The third place was an apartment. Not ideal, she knew, because she'd have to move once Thomas was old enough to want to start exploring outside, but it was clean and almost new and it had views around the next-door building to the harbour. Nathan was worried about the balcony. It gave him bad vibes, he told her. In less than a year Thomas would be toddling. 'What if a visitor one day leaves the door open accidentally and he manages to climb up on it? You're three floors up.'

Tessa shuddered. She took Thomas off Nathan and hugged him to her chest tightly.

The last place looked a little scruffy from the street but a couple of coats of paint on the inside would cheer it up amazingly, she thought, and the landlord had told her she could deduct the cost of materials from her rent. 'It's quiet,' she said, looking round. They were close to the road but the house was solidly built and she couldn't hear the traffic.

Nathan checked the foundations and looked under the house and in the ceiling and he knocked at the walls and opened and shut the doors and inspected cupboards and checked the hot water supply. She trailed after him, carrying Thomas, her enthusiasm growing as he seemed to be finding nothing wrong.

'I could grow my tomatoes here,' she said, indicating a sunny area against the side fence. 'And I could put a sandpit by the washing line when Thomas is a little older. There's plenty of room.'

'It's not a good neighbourhood.' Nathan looked at his watch. 'I don't like this place. It's not right for you. It's too far from the hospital and it's overpriced. Wait for something better to come along.'

'That might take months.' She looked around the yard. 'I don't mind driving a bit extra to work, in fact the more I see of this place the more I like it. And I'm renting, not buying. If it doesn't work out I can move in a year.'

'It's not good enough for you.' He put his hand around her back and steered her through the house. 'Forget it.'

Tessa was surprised he was so quick to be dismissive. 'I can't believe you're not desperate to get rid of us,' she said, after they'd driven around the agents and handed back all the keys. 'You're stuck with us for another week at least now. I would have taken that last place if you hadn't been with me.'

'I don't understand why you think you have to move.' He slowed and turned into the car park of the city supermarket where Tessa preferred to shop. 'Why the hurry? Is it so awful in Khandallah?' he asked, carrying Thomas while she selected a trolley.

'No.' Now it was her turn to be exasperated. She went ahead of him, choosing vegetables. 'But I have to find somewhere before I go back to work because after that I won't have time for looking and arranging the moving. As it is now, I'm already going to have to delay work one more week, possibly two. Yes, I know you think I should be leaving it much longer,' she said wearily, catching his frowning look, 'but we both know I can't keep putting it off indefinitely. Plus…' She looked around, searching for tomatoes for the lasagne she was planning. The supermarket tomatoes were hard and thick-skinned and they had no scent and they were terrifyingly expensive, but she had no choice but to select a few. She missed her vegetable garden terribly. '…You can't pretend we're not cramping your style.'

Since coming to live with him, she'd discovered she had seriously underestimated Nathan's social life. Apart from bed and breakfast he was virtually never home. 'I don't even know why we're buying food for you,' she mumbled, going through the parsley and oregano to find the freshest-looking bunches at the back. 'You'll probably be out every night again.'

Nathan worked a lot of nights of course, but instead of studying or catching up on sleep every other night, which was what she had to do to survive her own roster when she was working full time, he mostly came home only to shower and change before going out again. She always asked if he was meeting Georgette but he never was. Mostly it was a different woman each night. And she'd worried that he was lonely! 'You were out for dinner three nights last week. And I know we're cramping your style because you've never stayed away overnight or brought any of your dates back to the house.'

'Keeping track?'

'Not deliberately.' She moved fast down the next aisle, stopping only to toss in a few bottles of nappy soak. 'But I could hardly not notice. Thomas' bedroom looks over the carport and I'm up to him at least twice every night.' She picked up baking ingredients in the next aisle, then cleaning stuff from the next. 'It would be obvious if your car wasn't there.'

For a change there were no queues and they went straight through to a checkout operator. Nathan waited until they were outside the supermarket and on the way back to the car with the groceries. 'What makes you think I'd be doing anything different if you weren't staying?'

'You're a man, aren't you?' The observation earned her a swift, narrowed look before Nathan fastened Thomas back into his capsule, but she didn't flinch. He was her friend and she loved him but that didn't blinker her to life's little realities. She finished packing the bags into the back of Nathan's car then avoided his eyes when he opened her door for her. 'Why would you bother asking them out if you don't want to sleep with them?'

'Maybe I need to go out with them to discover if I want that.'

'I shouldn't have thought you needed to take out Claire to find that out.' She fastened her seat belt. She'd met the midwife at the hospital that week and had discovered that she and Nathan had had a very enjoyable night out at a restaurant. When they were waiting to exit the car park she added, 'I got the impression she would have been more than willing to come home with you. Only you didn't ask.'

She saw his hands clench the steering wheel but he was silent on the drive home and he parked quietly in the carport and turned off the engine in smooth, controlled movements. 'What are you saying?' His voice now was tight, threaded with a tension she didn't understand, and his green eyes surveyed her coolly. 'That if I have sex with Claire you won't move out?'

Nathan had been a little distant with her these past two

weeks. She'd noticed it but she'd put it down to him taking time to get adjusted to having someone living in his house. But they hadn't argued and aside from the night he'd talked her into coming to the house, this sort of verbal spat wasn't normal for them and it made her uneasy.

'Maybe not in such a hurry,' she said, trying to keep her tone conciliatory. 'I wouldn't feel so bad about interfering in your life.'

'And you wouldn't care about that?'

She opened her door and got out and he did the same and she looked at him over the roof of the Audi. 'About interfering?'

'About Claire spending the night here.'

'Why would I?' She opened Thomas' door with a vicious tug. 'I think you two would make a great couple.' She avoided saying she wouldn't care because that wouldn't be true. She liked the midwife a lot, enough to ask her to be with her for Thomas' birth, but liking her and wanting her to be with Nathan were different things. And it wasn't that she was being possessive, she told herself, jerkily unfastening the buckle and then the straps holding him in the capsule. But she was worried that Nathan might be using the other woman, all the other women, as a way of avoiding confronting his feelings for Georgette. 'It's your house,' she pointed out, under her breath, to herself as much as to him. 'I'm only visiting.'

'Perhaps I'm old enough now that the idea of casual sex seems soulless?' He was right behind her and when she lifted Thomas, he took him off her. 'Perhaps I find sex meaningless unless it involves emotional intimacy?'

'If that's true, then it's commendable.' His regard had gone from cool to cold and Tessa, chilled by it, glared back at him. Thomas had dropped off to sleep in the car and he didn't wake in Nathan's arms. She adjusted his blanket slightly around his face. 'Unusual,' she conceded tightly, 'and a little hard to believe considering you seem to go through women at a rate of at least three per week which isn't exactly giving you long with each one to establish anything like intimacy. Plus I doubt there are many men in the world who wouldn't crawl over broken glass to get a woman like Claire into bed. But your restraint is admirable. Simon's tongue used to almost hang out on the floor whenever Claire came to the house.'

Nathan's expression darkened. 'Don't ever,' he said tightly, '*ever*, judge me by Simon's standards.'

He carried Thomas in to the house ahead of her and Tessa, her hands shaking, collected the groceries slowly, delaying the time when she'd have to confront him again. When she finally walked inside, he was in the bedroom finishing changing Thomas. Without looking at her, he transferred him from his changing table and settled him into the cot. She turned her back and went into the main room and when he came out, with her throat thick with dread she said, 'How much do you know?'

'How much do you think?'

Tessa felt sick. Twice a year, every year, Simon had flown up to Auckland for reunion long weekends with a group of old friends from boarding school. There was always a lot of drinking and plenty of partying and she knew, by looking at his face and by the roses he used to bring her and by how thoughtful and attentive he was to her after those trips, that he'd been with other women. Nathan hadn't gone as religiously to all the Auckland weekends as Simon had, but he would have been at several of them. Obviously Simon hadn't always been discreet.

'So was it just those boys' weekends away or am I the proverbial last to know?' she asked painfully. 'Were there others at other times?'

'Why are you asking me that?' Nathan looked grim. He went to the window overlooking the pool, then to the opposite one, then to the other side of the room. 'I don't know. He wouldn't have confessed to me. He knew what I thought. How long have you known?'

'Straight away each time I suspect. I didn't ask but I knew he felt guilty about something.'

'*And you stayed with him?*'

'There's a difference between not minding something and understanding it and forgiving it.' Her legs felt weak and she held on to the bench to support herself. 'Boys will be boys and all that. It was only twice a year and since his hangover used to last days when he got home I imagine he was drunk most of the time…'

'Don't.' He sounded furious. 'Don't ever justify his behaviour to me. And never, never assume we're all the same.'

'All I said was that I was worried Thomas and I are disrupting your life. How did we get on to Simon?'

'Because everything with us will always come back to Simon. That's the way life is.' But he stopped then, stopped prowling around the room the way, and looked at her. 'God.' He ran a hand through his hair, his expression frustrated. 'I'm sorry. I didn't mean to say anything about those weekends. Ever.'

'It doesn't matter. I've forgiven him.' He'd left his hair spiked a little at the front and she had to damp down the urge to smooth it back for him. 'I get the feeling you haven't and I feel bad about that. I never wanted to come between your friendship. I wish things could have been different for all of us.'

'How different?'

Tessa was unsure now. 'Well, I wish that Simon had wanted Thomas enough to stay with me and make a family and that we could have got married and you could have been Simon's best man and that you and Georgette were together...'

Nathan made a harsh, dismissive sound. 'How many times do I have to tell you I'm not involved with Georgette before you'll believe me?'

'Whoever it is then,' she said quickly. 'Claire or whoever. Whoever it is your mother was talking about that day...'

Nathan swore under his breath. 'For God's sake, Tessa, are you really this stupid? Mum meant you. She assumed I had feelings for you.'

'*Me?*' Tessa almost yelped the word but then she slowly deflated. 'Oh, I see.' She felt silly. 'Oh, I'm sorry. That makes a bizarre sort of sense I suppose. It must have seemed strange to them when you asked her to take me from the hospital and with me moving in here?' She gestured around and faded out. 'I would have sorted it out immediately if I'd realised. This must all have been confusing for them then. You've explained I take it?'

'What would I need to explain?'

'That you don't have feelings for me,' she said awkwardly.

He tilted his head slightly. 'You believe that, do you?'

Her breath jammed, momentarily, in her throat. 'Why not since it's the truth?'

But he ignored that. 'You're right, that it's not surprising she misunderstood. Simon doesn't seem to be coming back and you and I have known each other a long time.'

'Almost six years.'

'We get on.'

'Very well.'

'You like living here.'

'I love living here.' Moving automatically, she went to the bags she'd left on the breakfast bar and started slowly unpacking them. 'Staying here, rather.' She took the cold things and the vegetables to the fridge and stacked them inside. 'It's going to be a wrench leaving.'

'We work well together.'

'We always have.' She piled baby wipes and the nappy soak on the floor separately and unpacked the dry goods into Nathan's pantry.

'We might even set up in the same private practice in a few years' time.'

'Really?' She straightened with a big smile. They hadn't talked about that before. She was overwhelmed. 'That would be so much fun. I'd love that.'

'It would make sense for us to get married.'

The last shopping bag slipped out of her hands and crashed to the floor. Luckily it held only laundry powder and toiletries and cleaning materials, but she barely noticed. Heedless of the mess she gasped at first then, when she saw he was serious, she started to laugh.

'I'm not joking,' he said tersely. 'It makes perfect sense.'

'Maybe a psychiatrist could work it out.' She laughed harder. 'Oh, God. I'm sorry.' She tried to catch her breath. 'Nathan, you have to know you are seriously nuts…'

'I'll adopt Thomas. We'll have to look into the legalities of that and no doubt we'll need Simon's signature somewhere along the way but my solicitor should be able to sort out the details. I realise you don't love me apart from as a friend but love hasn't done you much good in the past.'

'Not done me much good?' She was laughing again. 'It's almost *killed* me!'

'All the more reason...'

'I love it.' Her eyes were running as if she was crying and she grabbed blindly for the roll of kitchen towels to clear them. 'This is such a great joke. I get a beautiful place to live, a swimming pool, freedom from money worries, a great husband and a wonderful father for Thomas. And you get...' She could barely get out the words, '...*me*!' Nathan looking so straight and serious and disapproving merely made it seem all the more funny. 'What a bargain! Why aren't there men queuing up?'

'Sex won't be an issue,' he said, conversationally, as if it was an entirely normal announcement to make. 'Since I'm pre-warned to your tricks.'

'*Sex*? You want sex as well? With me? Oh, Nathan.' Tessa had almost sobered but now she started laughing again. 'You need help. You seriously need help. I have to go to the bathroom.' She slipped off the stool and held her stomach where it was sore from laughing. 'Before I wet myself. But always remember that I think you're the sweetest man in the world. Completely mad, but sweet. Rest assured that even at my lowest moments I promise not to take advantage of your knight in shining armour complex, but I do love you for it.' She patted his shoulder and walked carefully away. 'Very much.'

Her breasts were sore and so after the bathroom she looked in on Thomas. He was awake and smiling and he'd worked his arms free and he was waving them around and she lifted him out and they played with the mobile

Nathan's sister had bought him and she unbuttoned herself.

Nathan came to the door and lounged against the frame and watched her broodingly until she finished. She tidied herself up and stood up and rubbed Thomas' back gently, clucking to him as she carried him around the window, all the while casting Nathan quick, speculative looks, hoping he was over whatever flush of madness had possessed him earlier. But he looked on silently.

Eventually she sighed. 'You know it's ridiculous.'

'Because you can't think of anybody taking Simon's place?'

'Because of everything.'

'I think we'd be happy together.'

'I expect I'd be ecstatic. Until it all falls apart, that is. Then I'd be a wreck.'

She made to walk past him, but he caught her around the waist and pulled her against him. 'It wouldn't fall apart,' he growled. 'And at least I'd be faithful.' Nathan had kissed her plenty of times. And she'd kissed him. Socially. Always chastely. But there was nothing, absolutely nothing, chaste about the slide of his tongue against her lips. Tessa's brain scrambled. She gasped and Nathan took immediate, dizzying advantage of her open mouth. Her legs sagged a little, turned weak, and he shifted slightly, murmured something, kissed her throat and pressed her back into the wall, sliding a hand up her free side, where she wasn't holding Thomas, to cup her breast.

She felt an arch of sweetness sing through her body and she closed her eyes and dragged in a deep breath. His mouth came back to hers and she found herself unconsciously widening hers and shifting her legs to accommodate the demanding intrusion of his thigh, responding to the urgent thrust of his tongue with a small, tentative movement of her own. He said something, but deafened by the pounding of her pulse in her ears she couldn't hear what. Seconds later he lifted his head and spoke again but she didn't hear him again, and then he took away his mouth and moved his hand and finally released her.

She was trembling. With shock, she told herself numbly, not resisting when he gently extricated Thomas from her grasp. Shock that Nathan could have kissed her like that. 'You shouldn't do that when I'm holding him,' she said numbly. 'I could have dropped him.'

He lifted Thomas. 'I'll remember next time.'

She was still finding it hard to breathe. 'I don't think there should be a next time.'

'Why not? You liked it.' He manoeuvred Thomas to free up a hand and used it to hold her face. 'Don't deny it,' he warned, when she started to argue. 'You're hot.' The hand moved to her throat. 'And your heart's racing. Why did you tell me you never get aroused?'

'I'm not. It's shock. Remember I also told you I can fake anything.' She slapped away the hand that went to probe her breast. She already knew from how they felt that her nipples were tight. Being touched didn't normally make that happen, she generally felt nothing at all outside of exasperation, but they must be like this now because she was breast-feeding. Her breasts had grown sensitive because of that. And the room was hot, the sun had been coming in all morning, so of course she was flushed. And her heart was pounding like crazy out of panic, she knew. 'I'm an expert, remember.' She put out her arms. 'May I have my son back please?'

He passed Thomas across. 'I'm going out.' She'd annoyed him again now, she saw, judging from the tight set of his jaw. But he would have to deal with that. She thought it bizarre that they could go six years without ever exchanging an angry word only to have a day where they did nothing but argue. Well, almost nothing. She felt herself colouring again.

'I'll be late,' he added, making it sound like a growl. 'Don't make dinner for me. In fact, don't ever make dinner for me. And stop cleaning and washing and ironing my shirts. You're a guest, not my maid. I can take care of myself. And don't think, Tessa, that this conversation is over, because it hasn't even begun yet.'

'Are you meeting Claire?'

She hadn't meant to ask that, she couldn't believe that she'd followed him and that the words had burst out of her like that, but once she'd said it she couldn't do anything but stand there, sick to the stomach, holding Thomas and waiting while Nathan turned around at the front door.

'Don't you dare,' he said tightly, 'don't you bloody dare tell me again that you think we'd make a great couple.'

'I wasn't going to say that…' she protested. But he was already gone, the door shut tight behind him.

chapter nine

Nathan worked out fairly quickly that Tessa had decided his proposal constituted a mental aberration on his part and that she was going to deal with it by pretending kindly that it, and the kiss, had never happened. She was nervous the first day afterwards, but that faded when she saw he wasn't going to push her and by the end of the week she was almost back to her normal self with him. He said almost because he knew there had been a shift in their relationship. She was slightly self-conscious with him and her carelessness had gone. But he didn't seem to have done any permanent damage to their relationship.

He knew he should be relieved about that, but mostly what he felt was frustration.

Trying to distract himself hadn't worked. Taking out eight different women in three weeks had taught him only that neither his brain nor his body would accept any substitute for Tessa. But he'd never intended asking her to marry him. That hadn't been part of the plan. Not that there'd been one. Apart from the one where he was going to stay at least five kilometres away from her at all times. That hadn't worked.

She'd needed help with her shopping he rationalised. And he couldn't have seen her homeless.

There'd been one other strategy of course. The one where they would have a brief affair and he'd get the physical obsession out of his system and then they'd decide together to go back to being friends again forever.

Only he was old enough to know that life was never

that uncomplicated.

And after her revelations about how she'd been hurt in the past by men wanting only sex he'd known he couldn't ever think about doing that to her. He wasn't ready to let her write him off as another bad experience.

The timing wasn't right. For the next year until he earned his first consultant position he'd be working long hours at the hospital. But Tessa, of all people, would understand that and she'd know that the future would be better. Just as he'd always understand the demands of her own career.

The idea of having Tessa legally tied down was astonishingly compelling. For every reason he'd outlined to her. Not only because it was the only way he was going to get any relief from the constant urge to throw her over his shoulder and carry her to the nearest bed without having to put up with a lifetime of grief from his conscience.

He pulled into the car park and collected the mail before approaching the house. Tessa was in the kitchen eating one of her chocolate deserts but whatever was cooking on the stove was fragrant with lemon grass and chillies. She looked up with a gratifyingly pleased smile when he walked in. 'You're early,' she exclaimed. She put down her dessert and turned off the heat under the pot and came over and kissed his cheek. 'Does that mean you're going to be in for tea or do you have a date? How was your weekend?'

'In,' Nathan said shortly, not returning her kiss. It had been a warm day and her shorts were very short and to try and stop the evening becoming more complicated than it was already, he averted his eyes from the long expanse of thigh she was exposing. 'And the weekend was good.

Busy, we had a lot of admissions, but there weren't any major problems.' His gaze tracked to the rack of pressed shirts by the door and he stared at it for a few seconds before he gritted his teeth. 'Tessa…'

'I wish you'd stop going on about it,' she interrupted. 'It only takes five minutes and I had the iron out anyway to do my own things. I don't mind. Most men would be grateful…'

'Stop doing it.' He was going to have to take them to the laundry before she got to them, he realised. 'The only thing we agreed you were going to do was the garden design. I hate the thought that you're slaving away here doing menial chores when I'm at work.'

'It's not slaving and you're mad. You're the one doing the slaving, at work, for me, remember. You're covering for me being away. Washing and ironing a few shirts is nothing in comparison. Most men would assume I was going to do it.'

'But then we've already established that I'm not most men,' he said grimly. He sorted through the mail. 'For you.' He frowned at the express-post envelope before handing that and another one over. 'Plus they've sent you another lottery one.' She'd received a similar envelope the previous week. That one had told her that she'd won a prize in a foreign lottery she'd never entered or heard of and that it would only cost her thirty-nine dollars and ninety-nine cents to claim her large prize. He'd stopped her as she was writing out the cheque. 'Don't you dare,' he added warningly, catching her thoughtful look. 'Use your brain. Nobody ever sends anybody free money.'

'I don't know about that.' She spoke slowly as she inspected the contents of the bigger envelope. 'I think you might be wrong.' Her eyes huge, she showed him a cheque. A big cheque. 'I can't believe this,' she murmured. 'Some lawyer really has sent me money. Maybe I did win that lottery?' But her eyes scanned the first few lines of the accompanying note and he saw the colour drain out of her face.

'Tessa?'

'It's from Simon's mother and father.' She moved away from him and sank on to a stool at the breakfast bar. The cheque fell to the floor and she left it there. She read to the end of the note, then crushed the edges of it in her fingers and stared straight ahead. 'I sent them each a photo of Thomas a few days after he was born. I wrote to Simon's mother that if she wanted to see him, I'd be happy to fly up to bring Thomas to visit her.'

'And they got together and sent you a big cheque and said forget it.'

Nathan's voice was flat. He was making a statement, not asking her a question, and Tessa's numbed look up told him he'd surprised her. Nothing about it surprised him though. He only wished he'd known what she'd done because that way he might at least have been able to warn her in advance. 'What else?'

'The letter's from a lawyer. It says…' Her face crumpled as she passed it to him. 'There's lots of legal talk.'

He scanned the letter. 'They're offering a gift as a gesture of goodwill and final settlement without prejudice.'

She had her face in her hands. In a muffled voice she said, 'Which sounds as if it means that Thomas isn't going to have any grandparents.'

'Don't take it personally.' Nathan was grim. 'They're the ones with the problem.'

'Simon said they wouldn't be interested but I didn't

believe him. I thought there was a real chance Thomas was going to have a proper family. There's nobody on my side, no one at all. All he has is me.'

'Simon hasn't signed this. I doubt he even knows. And they're not denying his paternity.'

'Which makes it worse. They know he's their grandchild but they don't want anything to do with him. How can people be like this?' She looked devastated. 'How can they be so cold? He's a tiny little baby. How can they reject him without even meeting him? If they could only see how beautiful he is, they wouldn't be able to…Nathan, what if something happens to me?'

Tears spilled out of her eyes and trickled down her cheek but she seemed oblivious. 'What if Simon never comes home and something bad happens to me? Thomas won't have anybody. He'll be like I was, only he'll be too young to look after himself. What will happen to him? Will they put him in a home? Oh, God. What if people are horrible to him…?'

In six years, Nathan had never seen her cry about her own life. He'd seen her tearful at work in the face of the rare tragedies they sometimes had to confront, but not about herself. Not when her engagement had ended, not when Simon had left, not when she was in labour, not even that night when he'd had to tell her that Simon didn't sound as if he was coming back. He'd seen her holding back sobs on her first night home from the hospital but her control had been rigid and she hadn't let them out.

Watching her dissolve now and cry her heart out hurt him unbearably. He put his arms around her and cradled her into his chest and kissed and stroked her hair. 'Nothing bad is going to happen to either of you,' he murmured, holding her until her trembling and her tears finally eased then passing her a handful of tissues. 'Trust me, you don't need people like this in your life. If Thomas ever needs anything, I'll be here. I'll always look after him. I promise.'

Eventually she lifted her head away and rubbed her reddened eyes with the heels of her hands. She blew her nose on the tissue she'd given him. 'Oh, God, Nathan. You've already done so much.'

'Only because I want to. He'll have me, Tessa. And my parents and Zoe too. I promise. We'll be a family for him and we'll look after him. We will never let any stranger take him away.'

Eventually she wiped her eyes again and lifted her head and whispered, 'Thank you.' Her breathing was still catchy but she reached up and kissed his cheek. 'There aren't words to tell you how grateful I am to you. This means more to me than anything else in the world.'

'Don't keep thanking me. It's too much.' He hated it. 'I haven't done anything I haven't wanted to do.' If she knew what else he wanted to do she wouldn't be grateful, she'd be running, he knew. He gestured to the cheque. 'Are you going to tear it up?'

'I want to but it's not mine, it belongs to Thomas.' Slowly, her movements jerky, she bent and picked it up. 'I'll invest it for him and one day I'll be able to tell him that it was a gift from his family.' Her voice was still raw from the effect of her crying. 'I've made a Thai curry for tea. There's plenty for both of us if you're hungry.'

'It smells great.' He didn't protest again about her cooking for him. That would have felt churlish after she'd been so upset. He sorted through the rest of the mail and the cheque caught his eye again. He would have been happy to see Tessa destroy it – he'd seen too well the effect on Simon of his family's neglect to wish those people on any child, let alone Thomas – but he understood Tessa's decision. One day Thomas might want to investigate his heritage and the knowledge that they'd acknowledged him even in this token way would surely be better than thinking he'd had no recognition whatsoever.

'And you're too modest.' Tessa looked around from the stove where she'd been adding rice to a pot. Her eyes remained a little swollen but her cornflower gaze was clearer now. 'You've done so much for us that I'll never be able to make up for it, but I promise one day I'll do my best to pay back some of it.'

'You can pay me back in total now by saying you'll marry me.'

'Not that again.' The way she rolled her eyes and smiled told him she thought he was joking, but at least now she seemed distracted from her earlier misery. 'Remind me, again, what would be in that for you? Aside from two extra people in your house, a load of extra expenses and a serious dimmer switch on your social life, that is.'

He came across and studied the fragrant curry appreciatively, then found himself lifting her dark hair aside to expose her neck. He put his mouth to the pale, scented skin at her neck and kissed her. 'I get you.'

Gratifyingly, he felt her shiver slightly before she stiffened. 'Oh, yes.' Her voice was husky. 'I remember. What a bargain.'

'I think so.' He shifted his mouth slightly and kissed her again and stroked his hand down her back. 'I like it that you haven't come before.' Her scent and the sweet delicacy of her skin went straight to his senses in a heady rush. 'I like it that the first time will be with me.'

She went rigid. 'Don't,' she whispered. 'Please.' She

lowered her head, but that only left more of her neck bare and he couldn't stop himself exploring it with his mouth. 'Why do you want to ruin everything?'

'It's not ruining, it's making it better.'

'We're fine as we are!'

'It's a fairy tale.' Quietly he reached around her and switched off both elements on the stove. Then he put his arms around her waist and drew her against him. She was stiff and resisting in his arms but her breathing had gone ragged again and when he tracked his mouth around to the side of her throat he could feel her pulse fluttering as fast as his. 'It isn't real. You only think it works because I hide things from you. This is honest. I want you to marry me and I want to look after you and I want to make love to you. Not right away, but slowly. I won't rush you, I'll take it one step at a time and you're going to be with me all the way.'

'Oh, God.' She sounded anguished. 'I thought…I *hoped* you were joking. I thought that was all part of your repair-my-ego project.'

He almost groaned. If only. 'I've never been more serious about anything in my life.'

'It won't work. I won't work. It's my fault. I've thought in the past with men that things are going to be different this time, only they never are. I don't want to disappoint you.' She tipped her head back and stared up at him. 'You'll end up frustrated and angry and then it'll be the same as with all the others and I'll lose you. We won't even be friends afterwards. I can't do it.' She shook her head. 'You mean too much to me.'

He brought his hands up to cup the undersides of her breasts and his world spun. 'I'm not going anywhere,' he assured her roughly. 'Whatever happens. Trust me.'

'I can't when you do things like this!' Tessa pushed his hands away and turned around in his arms. She stared up into his face and shivered a little when she saw how implacable he looked. 'It's hopeless. I promise you, you're wasting your time with me. Go – go see Claire and bring her back and get it out of your system and then when you don't want sex anymore, we'll be friends again and everything will be fine.'

But instead of being grateful that she was offering him that out, he looked angry. 'It won't, because it hasn't been fine for weeks. In reality, it probably hasn't been fine for years. I think at some, perhaps even sub-conscious level, we've been playing games to keep it that way and I've had enough. I don't want Claire. I don't want anyone but you. And stop seeing this as just sex. That's secondary…'

'It didn't feel secondary when you were holding me ten seconds ago.'

'If I could get rid of that by sleeping with anyone else, don't you think I'd have done that by now?' he demanded.

'You haven't tried too hard. Claire said she practically had to launch herself at you to get even a kiss goodnight.'

'It isn't Claire,' he pointed out icily, 'I want to kiss.'

'Which shows how stupid you are!' She closed her eyes and held the sides of her head with her hands and squeezed to try and ease the tension that was starting to throb there. 'Why do you have to make everything so complicated?'

'It's not complicated at all. Not now. It's far simpler than it's ever been.'

'Not for me,' Tessa pointed out shakily. 'It's not at all simple for me.' To her overwhelming relief, the baby intercom he'd brought for her crackled into life and she heard Thomas cry out and she had the best excuse in the world to turn away from him. Thomas was becoming less demanding in terms of frequency of feeds than he'd been as a new-born but he had become more efficient and she noticed he took more with every feed. His weight gain was good and the Plunket nurse who'd called in twice to visit him was pleased with him. He'd lost a few ounces initially, that was normal, but he was doing well now. Over the last two weeks he'd started sleeping three or four hours at a time through the night, instead of one or two, but because his weight was firmly within the right percentile in his growth chart she knew he was still getting enough nourishment.

'You're very good, aren't you?' Her hands were shaking, she saw, but she managed to smooth back his fair hair. 'You don't give me any trouble.' At eight weeks old he was smiling all the time and he seemed to recognise her and Nathan and he already had his own, happy little personality. 'You never growl at me and you never complain.'

'You were eating your pudding when I got home but you forgot to finish it.'

Tessa jumped at Nathan's voice. Her nervous gaze skittered to where he stood, dark and shadowed against the wall near the door.

'Yoghurt,' she corrected, focusing on the tub and spoon he held because that was infinitely easier than looking at him and thinking about what he'd said and what he wanted and how she'd shuddered when his mouth had touched her skin. It was impossible. She knew that. She'd survived Simon. Just. Nathan, she feared, would be the end of her. 'And it doesn't matter. I'll finish it later.'

'You shouldn't leave it sitting around once you've opened it,' he pointed out with a calmness she could only envy. 'The sugar and milk make it the perfect culture medium for bacteria. Another ten minutes could turn it deadly.'

'Put it in the fridge then.' She half-lifted Thomas, now firmly fastened on to her left breast to demonstrate why she wasn't interested at the moment. 'I can't eat it. My hands are busy.'

'Waste not, want not. I can see the best solution is for me to feed you.'

'I don't need to be fed. Throw it away if it makes you feel better. I don't care. I've plenty more. I bought a whole tray of them.' She looked away from him, turning deliberately back to her son, then twisted her face away, her mouth closed tightly when, ignoring her attempts to evade him, Nathan came around, crouched in front of her and put a spoonful of yoghurt up to her mouth.

'I don't want it.'

But he smiled. 'Open up.' He made train noises. 'Tell mummy to eat, Tom,' he instructed. 'Tell her she needs her pudding. Tell her not to be naughty when I'm going to all this trouble for her.'

Thomas, too busy feeding to do much more than stare wide-eyed at Tessa's tormentor, seemed unconcerned but Tessa herself felt a considerable amount of concern.

She felt her pulse thud when her eyes met and clung to Nathan's confusingly intent regard and when he proffered the laden spoon to her lips, since it seemed wiser than trying to stand up to him when he was clearly in the mood to taunt, she gave in and opened her mouth and let him feed her the dessert.

'Very nice,' she said, even to her ears sounding strained. 'Go away.'

'Not till you've had some more.' He put another spoonful into her mouth, then, when she'd swallowed that, another. 'He likes that,' he murmured.

'Yes.' Doing her best to fight the mesmerising spell Nathan, along with the intimate closed-curtained darkness of the room, seemed to be casting, she looked down at Thomas. 'He always does.'

'I can understand that,' he said softly. 'He's male after all.'

Tessa drew in a sharp breath. 'I don't think you should...'

'You don't think I should what? Hmm? Feed you?' He offered her another spoon of the dessert, put it into her open mouth, and she swallowed automatically then felt her face colour at his murmur of approval.

'I think we should both forget tonight. And I don't think you should be talking to me like this.'

'You're nervous.' He offered her another spoonful but she twisted her head at the last minute and instead of her mouth he touched it to the side of her cheek. He tutted at her. 'Am I so terrifying?'

'Yes. You're scaring me half to death,' she whispered. 'What are you doing?'

'Helping you eat your pudding.' He put the spoon back into the pot and used a finger to retrieve the yoghurt that must have stained her cheek then he put his finger into her mouth meaning she had to lick him with her tongue to retrieve the chocolate. 'You feed Thomas, I feed you,' he said quietly. 'It seems a fair exchange. Did that taste nice?'

'Mmm.' Tessa stared at him. Her eyes felt as if they'd grown huge and she felt hypnotised. She knew she should be fighting him, pushing him away, refusing to play the crazy games he seemed determined to play with her, but her body felt suddenly heavy and lazy, and her brain seemed incapable of telling her to do anything but stay exactly where she was.

'Want more?' He dipped his finger into the pot this time and offered her that and, helplessly, she let him put it into her mouth again, sucking, this time, to capture the last of the chocolate before he withdrew.

Thomas kicked against her stomach and released her breast and she lifted him, understanding what he wanted. 'I have to put him down now. He needs his sleep.'

'I'll help you.' Nathan slid her dress from her opposite shoulder, then, with gentle hands although she still gasped her shock at what he was doing, instead of simply closing the cup of her bra he slid down the straps and lowered it to completely expose her bare breasts.

Trembling strongly now, Tessa switched Thomas across to nestle down by her side, but when her hand lifted automatically to cover herself, Nathan stopped her.

'Leave it,' he instructed, capturing her hand and holding it away, stopping her concealing herself. 'I like looking at you.'

'No you don't.' Tessa made a soft, helpless sound. 'You don't like it. Usually you turn away.'

'Only because of what looking at you makes me want to do. I didn't want to scare you so much that you stopped trusting me.'

'It's too late.' She stared at him. 'I don't trust you any more.' Her skin burned where his eyes grazed her flesh but at the same time she revelled in the quickening in his breathing and the heat she could feel radiating from him because they told her that he wanted her. That should have been bad – she knew it was bad – dangerous even, but still the fear vied in her heart with something sickeningly like excitement.

'I'm only looking.' Nathan retrieved the spoon he'd

discarded and loaded it with yoghurt again and lifted it almost to the mouth she held obediently half-open for him, but he didn't give it to her. He tilted the spoon and let the yoghurt slide off.

A cool dollop landed on Tessa's bare breast, making her gasp.

'Oh, clumsy.' Instead of the spoon, Nathan used his finger to collect the chocolate, spreading it, as he did so, across the hardened tenderness of her nipple so that she shivered and closed her eyes weakly. 'Sorry.'

She felt his finger at her mouth and she sucked again, panting gently, her heart seeming to beat so fast she feared for herself. 'Nathan…'

'It's all right.' She felt his fingers cup her breast and her eyes flew open as his head lowered.

The touch of his mouth at her breast, licking at the chocolate, sent strings of exquisite flame shooting across her skin. She twisted her head slowly away from him. 'I thought you didn't have a sweet tooth.'

'I have a taste for you.' He cupped the rounded weight of her breast tenderly in his palm, his tongue circling the tightened bud and then sliding over it and Tessa arched slightly, feeling the sudden deep drawing within her as her womb contracted in sympathy.

She made some sound, a small, yearning sound and Nathan looked up at her and his eyes seemed to burn her skin. She felt a movement and this time when he lowered his head his hand moved between her unresisting thighs inside her shorts and beneath the thin cotton of her underwear.

He kissed her breast and simultaneously slid one finger inside her. Tessa sucked in a shocked breath, caught off guard as much by the dizzying rush of sensation between her breast and his finger as much as by the shockingly intimate intrusion of the caress. Thomas, perhaps sensing her distraction, struggled against her other side, and as he wailed his bootie-covered feet kicked out against Nathan's jaw.

Thomas couldn't have hurt him, but Nathan, as if startled, drew back sharply. For a few moments he seem to freeze but then, capturing her son's little foot briefly, he kissed the heel of his bootie, then released him and released her and rose to his feet. Tessa, still dazed, mechanically altered Thomas' angle, lifting him on to her shoulder then stared numbly up at Nathan as his expression slowly drained of heat and turned impassive.

She moistened her parched lips. 'Nathan?' It came out as a soft, helpless plea.

'That's enough now,' he responded gruffly. He didn't look at her. 'I can't stay and not…' But he stopped. 'I have to go in to work.'

He was almost sick with self-contempt. The dizzying euphoria of finding her wet and knowing that he'd done that had sent him almost crazy. He'd been at best half a minute away from unfastening her clothes and lowering his mouth to follow the movement of his fingers when Thomas' kick had brought him to his senses. He'd been determined to take things slowly, to go delicately with Tessa. He was still determined to do that and he was appalled at how close his lack of self-control had brought him to ruining everything for her and for both of them.

Calling himself a dozen different kinds of idiot didn't help him feel any better about how far he'd pushed his luck, but at least getting out of there gave them both space to deal with it, Nathan acknowledged, his face grim as made his way outside. He knew he'd have a long hard road ahead of him to get her to trust him even fractionally again.

He'd lied about having to go back to the hospital. He wasn't on call. But that didn't mean he didn't have work to do when he got there, and he spent the rest of the night into the early hours of the morning in his office, at his desk, dictating machine in hand, working his way through a stack of notes that had been waiting his attention for weeks.

He got home a little after three and although Tessa had left the outside light on for him the rest of the house was in darkness. He rose deliberately early, skipped breakfast and his swim, and went straight into the hospital. He was on the ward by seven, his early arrival earning him surprised looks from the nurses on the main Gynae ward still busy receiving their hand-over from the night staff.

When he finally arrived home, very late on Tuesday evening, Tessa's car – the idea of exchanging cars for the rest of summer made sense to him yet she still refused to consider it – was there but there was no sign or sound of her or Thomas and he guessed they'd already gone to bed.

It had been a long, sultry day and although the wind was coming up now it was still warm and he changed out of his work clothes and dived into the pool.

He saw lights go on a while later in the house and when he finally finished his lengths and hauled himself out of the water he saw Tessa, in a long pink, cotton nightie, so well-washed it was almost transparent, go to the fridge in his kitchen and pour herself a glass of mixed juice and water.

He wrapped a towel around his hips and sluiced the water from his chest and arms while he watched her take a few long swallows, his eyes devouring every detail of the shadowy outline of her luscious curves beneath the thinness of her gown.

chapter ten

He walked slowly to the door but still oblivious to him she turned and walked through from the kitchen into the living area. She stretched then crouched then stretched again and he frowned as he saw her rubbing at her lower back with her hand as if her muscles were causing her pain again.

He opened the sliding door into the kitchen. Several times in her first days at the house he'd done his best to alleviate her discomfort with massage. He hadn't exactly found the exercise unpleasant – far from it – and he'd suffered for that, but his motives had been as pure as they could have been in the circumstances and his touch had never been anything but strictly therapeutic. But one night she'd informed him that all her discomfort was gone and that there was no need for him to do anything more.

He'd wondered if he'd hurt her and she didn't feel she could tell him. But since she'd been uncomfortable when he'd tried to question her on it, he'd left it alone.

Whatever her reasons for asking him to stop the massages, her gesture now with her hand suggested that her back pain had returned again. Concerned, he moved into the kitchen then followed her. 'Tessa…?' If he could help then he wanted to. 'Are you OK? Is your back hurting? I saw you holding yourself…'

'Nathan!' She'd been stretching over the back of one of his sofas, reading the open TV guide at the same time on the cushions, but now she straightened and whirled around. The startled, almost panicked way her beautiful eyes scanned his chest then dropped to the towel at his waist revealed she hadn't heard him in the pool. 'I didn't realise you were home.'

'It's been a long shift. I needed the exercise. Are you in pain?'

'No. Not at all.' But her skin flushed and her eyes lowered and she spoke so quickly he didn't believe her.

'Let me at least examine you.' He ignored the arm she held out. 'Don't be silly.' He captured her hand. 'I won't hurt you. I won't do anything but touch your back. Let me feel why you're hurting.'

'It's nothing,' she protested, but he frowned again and turned her around.

'You're stiff as a board,' he said tightly, doing his best to assess the uneven state of her muscles through her nightie. 'Your muscles are in spasm and you're pulling to one side. Lift this up,' he added impatiently, dragging up the gown where it hindered his examination. Gathering it at her waist, he held it there with his forearm and bent lower. She was bare beneath the gown, and her wiggles told him she was self-conscious about that, but the medical part of his brain took over and let his concentration on his examination suppress the distraction of her nudity.

'Bend here,' he ordered, instructing her to move different ways so he could assess how limited her movements were by the pain. 'Stop fighting,' he added irritably when she stiffened beneath his hands again as he moved her upright again. 'Let me feel properly. I can help you.'

'It would help me more if you didn't keep ordering me about,' she complained, although she had, finally at least, stopped resisting him, and let the sofa take her weight.

Nathan shook his head. 'You're a terrible patient,' he

murmured. 'Has anyone ever told you that?'

'You,' she grumbled. 'Lots of times. Ouch!'

'Sorry.' But he smiled. He preferred her fighting any day to subdued and self-conscious. 'Is that any better now?'

'Marginally.' But she sounded annoyed about it and when he let her nightie slide down to cover her and helped her around to face him again, her face was flushed.

'Don't look at me like that, it was your fault,' he protested. 'If you hadn't let it go so long you wouldn't have been so bad. Why didn't you tell me you were in pain again?'

'Because I didn't want to put you to any trouble,' she told him stiffly. 'Thank you but may I go back to bed now, please?'

'In a minute.' Nathan stepped between her and escape. He put a finger under her stiff chin and tilted her head up, eyeing her assessingly. 'Did I hurt you before? Is that why you didn't say anything?'

'You didn't hurt me.'

'Then why suffer?'

'There is nothing to be gained by this discussion.' She looked past him over his shoulder, her expression set. 'I need to go to my room now.'

'And I told you that you can have it in a minute,' he told her gruffly. 'Tessa…'

'I have nothing to say to you,' she interjected stonily.

'Humour me.' He was bemused. 'All I was doing was trying to relieve your pain. What did I get wrong?'

'It wasn't you, it was me.' She glared at him, her blue eyes angry. 'It was your fault. You made me think of other things.'

'Like what?'

She screwed up her mouth for a few seconds then burst out, 'I didn't know how anything could be better than what you were doing ordinarily. I kept wondering how an erotic massage could possibly be an improvement and I was worried that one day, out of curiosity, I might ask you to try it out. After the way you've been carrying on lately, I was worried that you might actually take me seriously.'

'Why would you even think about asking for that?' he asked numbly. 'You keep saying you don't want it to be like that with us.'

'I know. And I mean it!' Blue sparks seem to shower from her eyes. 'That's what makes it so horrible.'

But something jarred. 'Wait a minute, you stopped wanting a massage within a week or so of moving into the house. Way before I kissed you.'

'I started thinking about it that first night I was home after Thomas.' He felt as if he was dragging the words out of her. 'The first time you did my back for me.'

He stared at her. 'You had the cheek on your first night here to tell me you were glad there'd never be any sex in our relationship when all the time you'd been fantasising about asking me for an erotic massage?'

'It wasn't fantasising…'

'Do you have any idea of the hell you put me though by saying that?'

'It couldn't have been any worse than what you're doing to me now,' she cried. 'And what you did to me last night. Do you think my life has been easy lately? I didn't sleep a wink last night!'

'Then it's time we got you a lot more relaxed.' He slid one arm around her back and another under her thighs and when she didn't struggle, when she let him pick her up, he carried her into his bedroom and pulled back the covers and put her on the bed. He turned on a lamp. 'I don't have a table, so the bed will have to do. Take off your clothes,' he ordered, before pulling the door closed. He checked on Thomas but the baby was fast asleep and he watched him quietly for few, introspective moments before going to collect the intercom from the main room along with the almond oil he'd used before on Tessa's back.

Tessa hadn't been able to bring herself to do anything but sit exactly where he'd left her and when Nathan opened the door and walked in she looked up slowly. He still wore a towel around his hips from his swim but his magnificent shoulders and chest were bare and she felt her breath catch. 'Nathan, you know I won't…'

'I don't expect anything but for you to enjoy it. You don't have to perform, it's not an exam. If you're staying you can stop me whenever you want but for now you have to undress.'

Tessa's eyes tracked his movements around the room. He put Thomas' baby intercom on the dressing table beside the bed along with the oil and he turned the lamp away from the bed to dim the light. 'It's not fair if it's always me,' she said quietly. 'Will you teach me what to do too?'

'That's not a good idea.' He let their eyes meet briefly. 'Not yet.'

She felt herself colour slightly. It was ridiculous, this fear, she knew, because it was only a massage and he'd said it himself, he didn't expect her to do anything. But still this was Nathan and that increased the stakes immeasurably and she turned away from him to undress, flushing as much with nerves as with self-consciousness.

In a sweeping movement she shed her nightie and arranged herself front down on the bed, her head on her bent arms, her legs together behind her. 'Is this all right?' she asked, her voice muffled by her hands and the bedding.

'It's good.' Nathan gathered her hair at her nape then twisted it underneath her and with an almost impersonal air he kissed the back of her neck. 'Concentrate on keeping your breathing slow and deep. Are you warm enough?'

'Very.' The sun had been coming into the room all afternoon.

He started the same way he always did, with oiled hands making smooth, stroking movements across her back, radiating from her spine, growing gradually firmer and extending the strokes to make them longer as she grew used to it. Her buttocks were bare and she was self-conscious about that at first, but when she realised he was treating them merely as an extension of her back, she felt herself relaxing.

Nathan moved from her back to her neck then lower to thoroughly massage her legs and feet. He rested his hands on her toes. 'Turn over,' he ordered quietly.

Beneath the languid torpor induced by the massage, Tessa felt a pang of anxiety. 'Won't the oil stain the sheets?'

'I don't care.'

She hesitated for a few seconds, then slowly, very slowly, she closed her eyes and rolled over on to her back. Nathan stayed at her feet. He massaged her toes and the top of her feet then her ankles and heels and in long, slow, drugging strokes he moved up her legs to her knees and then the tops of her thighs and then lightly, his fingers only brushing, to her inner thighs. She felt herself tensing again. Because she couldn't in a million years have looked at him, she kept her eyes squeezed shut but instead of the intimacy she was steeling herself for, his fingers slid lightly around the border of where her underwear would have been if she'd been wearing any, to her tummy.

He made slow, circular strokes with his hands, using them in tandem, one after the other. The sensation was deeply relaxing and she felt the tension in her face and her throat ease and she stopped squeezing her eyes shut and let them close heavily on their own. His fingers trailed so lightly over her breasts she barely felt them and then he worked her shoulders and down each arm in turn to her hands his strokes growing lighter and lighter as he reached her fingers until he moved up her arms again and she could barely feel him.

'I feel like a lump of well-kneaded dough in the hands of an expert baker,' she murmured, thinking he was finishing now. 'I'm so sleepy…'

But the light trace of his fingers across her breasts again made her break off with a gasp. 'Oh.'

He shushed her softly but she gasped again at the exquisite sensation in her nipples as his fingers, with the lightest of touches, gently outlined the fullness of each breast then traced each quadrant and returned to tease the tightened peaks. She squeezed her eyes shut again, suddenly not sleepy at all. 'Nathan…'

'Are they sore?'

'Not sore.' She felt breathless. 'Strange. Tingly.'

'They're beautiful.' Her skin heated in the spoke-like patterns traced by his fingers as he caressed every centimetre of her skin, finishing each time at the hard, tightened nub of her nipple. He caught the raised crests between his thumb and forefinger and squeezed softly, and she gasped again. She felt her hips lifting slightly and her breathing starting to come soft and fast and without conscious thought she shifted her legs again, widening them slightly.

As if the movements of her body gave him some signal, Nathan's hands drifted lower, across her tummy again but lighter this time and without pausing before he moved lower. He moved his thumbs to the inner part of her thighs and applied gentle pressure and Tessa, breathless now, let them open a little more then let him quietly lift her left foot up to close to her bottom and bend her knee flat against the bed.

He stroked her inner thigh then his fingers, so lightly it might have been accidental. Always before she'd found any touch in that area irritating rather than pleasing but now Tessa felt every muscle tightening and straining forward in desperation to capture more of that elusive teasing touch.

Tense with expectation, she arched her hips off the bed again, but Nathan, shushing her again quietly when she tried to protest, put a gentle hand on her stomach and pushed her back into the bed. He lifted and separated her other leg then stroked her the same way, caressing her thigh in long, very light strokes that occasionally drifted higher. Each time his fingers brushed her she quivered.

She felt sweat break out all over her body. 'Please,' she finally whispered brokenly when the straining and the pressure had grown unbearable.

She didn't know what she wanted him to do, only that she'd never felt anything like this tension before. 'Nathan...'

'Breathe,' he ordered. 'Deep and regular.'

Tessa tried. She tried to keep breathing but the air kept catching in her throat before it got anywhere near her lungs. At the next fleeting brush of his fingers she panted and lifted her hips again but Nathan pushed her back, only this time when she settled, instead of returning to stroking her legs he let his fingers drift lower from her tummy. He skimmed the tender flesh between her thighs and for the first time directly caressed the delicate folds between them.

She shuddered. She squeezed her eyes shut and held herself rigidly still, every fibre of her consciousness focussed on his fingers as they gently parted her and held her open. So lightly she could almost have thought she'd imagined it, he touched her with one finger, then another. Then rhythmically but never in the same place twice, sometimes slipping inside her, sometimes outside, he moved them in tiny circular patterns, teasing her, sometimes stronger, sometimes lighter, sometimes in places that made her gasp but never long enough for her to understand what was happening to her before he returned to less tender spots, teasing her so that he drove her crazy and made her bite down hard on her lips lest she humiliate herself by screaming out in frustration.

'Tessa, sweetheart?' She felt Nathan move beside her and his hand slid up to her tummy again and when she dragged her eyes open he'd shifted from sitting on the bed to laying beside her. He was still wearing the towel and the fabric felt soft yet rough at the same time against her hip. Beneath his warmth, she could smell the musky scent of his skin. 'You're breathing too fast and you keep tensing up.' He rested his head on his bent arm and with his other he stroked across her midriff then up between her straining breasts to the scented hollow at the base of her throat and back again. 'Slow down. Relax. Concentrate on your breathing. Forget about what I'm doing.'

'*Forget what you're doing*?' She let out a broken, husky-sounding laugh. 'That's a joke, I take it.' She lifted one hand vaguely, but it felt heavy and the effort was too great and she let it fall back on to the bed. 'I can't…I've never felt like this, Nate. I'm not pretending.'

'I know.' He smoothed back her hair and kissed her temple. 'But try for me, hmm?' He drifted his hand over her breasts again, circling her nipples but only touching them teasingly at random and she felt her womb contract and her nipples strain almost painfully upwards.

'Deep breathing,' he murmured, letting one finger rub softly against one hardened bud. 'Concentrate. No tension.'

Tessa's hands curled into fists at her sides. She wanted to grab his hands and flatten them against her but slowly she made her hands uncurl. 'No tension.' She closed her eyes and repeated the words in her head like a mantra. 'That feels…amazing.'

'You are so incredibly sexy.'

'I'm not sexy at all.' Slowly, through the haze of befuddlement, she shook her head. 'That's the irony.'

'I could spend all night here,' he said softly. Briefly, painfully briefly, he held one nipple between his thumb and forefinger and squeezed softly and instantaneously the impulse seemed to trigger a shivering senstation all the way through her. Her thighs lifted again involuntarily and she brought her legs together, unable to stop herself squeezing them together.

'Nathan…'

'Shush, I know.' She felt the bed move as he shifted again and then he gently opened her legs and folded her knees again. She felt his fingers stroke across her breasts again then when she arched his hand slid to her tummy again to press her back into the bed before descending lower.

Murmuring reassurance, he gently parted her again then circled her with two fingers then slid one deep inside her and stroked her.

Tessa felt as if he'd given her an electric shock. She bit her lips to stop herself crying out but some sound must have escaped or she must have betrayed herself somehow else because his fingers stilled immediately and his other hand returned to her tummy and pressed her back and held her there firmly until she stopped resisting him and lay flat and got her breathing back under control.

'What was that?' she managed to say finally. 'Was it…'

'Not yet.' His palm against her stomach gentled. 'That was only a tingle. You have a G spot.'

'Oh my God.' The words came out brokenly. 'I didn't even know I had an A to F.'

He smiled, then lowered her head. 'Let's see if we can find them, shall we?'

Tessa didn't know what he was finding, but every tiny movement of his fingers felt incredible. She lay back, trying to concentrate on her breathing but she kept losing it but Nathan forced her to remember it by withdrawing his touch every time she held her breath and waiting until she dragged herself back from what felt like the edge of a precipice and found the discipline to drag in another breath. She couldn't believe that it could be this pleasurable to have someone touching her like this. The muscles of her legs went so taut that they started to tremble, and when he leaned against them and murmured for her to relax, she had to force them down.

She shut her eyes. She felt his fingers moving again, sliding fractionally higher and she gasped and although, fearful of him stopping again she kept perfectly still, inside she felt her pelvis straining upwards towards their teasing trail. Fresh prickles of sweat broke out across her face and chest. She could feel where she wanted him to touch, she could feel exactly where she wanted pressure, she squeezed her eyes shut and tried to will him, telepathically, to go straight there but instead he touched beside it and above it and around it, never exactly where she wanted until she thought she might die unless he found it.

Remembering that he would stop again if she held her breath, she tried desperately to concentrate on her lungs. In and out, she chanted, filling her chest and releasing the air in the rhythm of her words. In and out. But the slow, delicious movements of Nathan's fingers distracted her and made her gasp again and again and then finally, finally, almost as if by accident, he let a finger slide delicately over the tiny, quivering nub. She sucked in her breath and went rigid. He did nothing for a few, painful moments and then his finger moved again, repeating the tiny touch, so light it could have been a butterfly flitting across her skin, and then, when she strained so tensely upward it was as if she was trying to force herself towards the sky, he touched again and her whole world imploded.

She fell back into the bedding, panting for breath, not able to think, not able to see, aware only of the throbbing convulsions. She tried to draw her legs up then, roll away, but Nathan held her legs apart and slid his fingers inside her again to that place he'd touched earlier and, incredibly, when she'd thought she might never feel anything else, she felt another spasm and then another and another until, finally, Nathan folded the sheets around her and rolled her into them. He lay beside her and hugged her until the trembling started to ease and she could think again.

And then all she felt was unbearable tiredness. She knew she needed to open her eyes, but she couldn't bear to. She couldn't remember ever feeling so exhausted. She tried to move her legs but they felt as if they were encased in concrete. She managed a few words, vague murmurs, nothing intelligible even to her, but he stroked her hair and adjusted the blankets at her chin and hugged her outside the bedding and told her to sleep.

She slid immediately into a thick, dreamless slumber until a hand at her shoulder and Nathan's voice quietly saying her name over and over finally brought her round again. It was still dark apart from the light thrown out from the corner lamp and she sat up, confused and disorientated for those first waking moments and stared up at him.

'Sorry.' He had a cross, complaining Thomas in his arms and he waited until he was sure she was properly awake before passing him to her. 'I didn't want to wake you but he's been crying for you. I've changed him and taken him for a walk but he wants more.'

'I can't believe I slept through him crying.' She scrambled up in the bed and reached for Thomas, guilt-stricken that she hadn't heard him. She'd been a light sleeper since the birth – nature's way, she guessed, of making sure she didn't miss him waking – and she was appalled that Nathan had heard him before she had. She was naked still and Thomas fastened immediately to her breasts and his sniffles subsided as he began to drink. 'I'm sorry.' She could smell chlorine and she saw Nathan's hair was wet. 'You've been swimming again? What? What time is it?'

'Just before four. I'm going to try and get some sleep in the other room so I don't disturb you when I get up.'

He bent and kissed her and he touched Thomas' head briefly. 'I'll take the intercom again so I'll hear him later if he wakes. Sleep in as long as you want. Goodnight.'

''Night.' Thomas was demanding her attention so she responded absently, but when her son settled into his rhythm again, she stared after Nathan. Wide awake now, she could remember everything and she felt herself starting to flush. She heard water running in the spare bathroom, then she heard movement and then the door to the spare bedroom along the hall closed and then there was silence.

Worried that she might wake Nathan by walking past his room, she was tempted to keep Thomas with her when he'd finished feeding. But there was a risk he'd overheat with her, she knew, so finally when his eyelashes started to dust his cheeks, she kissed him gently and tiptoed to his room.

She spent a little while settling him into his cot and tucking in his blankets and waiting until she was sure he was properly settled. On her way back up the hallway she found herself stopping at the spare room. Without any conscious thought on her part, her hand went to the handle, and, carefully and quietly, she opened it. Nathan was asleep. His breathing was deep and regular and didn't alter when she crept into the room. The moon outside was only a few days past full and he'd left the blinds open and there was plenty of light. He was sprawled naked on top of the bed. He hadn't bothered getting under the covers and the swimmers and towel he'd been wearing were thrown in a heap on to the carpet.

She scooped them up and put them on one of the cane chairs by the window so the dampness wouldn't stain the polished floor. For a few minutes she simply studied him silently. He'd looked tired when he'd brought her Thomas, pale almost, and she felt guilty about that. He'd done everything for her, she acknowledged. He'd changed her life. For no return. She'd never known a more selfless lover.

And he was so beautiful. Oblivious to her own nakedness, she moved to the bed and crouched beside it. Softly, very softly, she touched his left shoulder and then she let her fingers drift lower, to his nipples, the same way she remembered him caressing her. The tiny nubs hardened immediately she touched them and she started a little, stunned that such a subtle touch, when he seemed so deeply asleep, could rouse such a response. Unable to resist, she bent her head and tenderly flicked each tight nipple with her tongue. Nathan stirred then, moved his leg slightly, and she froze. But he didn't wake.

When his breathing grew regular again she told herself she should be grateful for small mercies and she should leave but she couldn't stop her hand reaching out for his chest again and then it slid lower across his flat belly to the muscled strength of his thighs. Gathering confidence when his sleep seemed to deepen, not lighten, she let her hand gently surround the thick base of his penis. Experimentally she tightened her grip fractionally and she felt a rush of pleasure when the shaft began to thicken and lengthen.

She'd always taken the male response for granted but always before she'd touched only because she felt obliged to. It was a heady feeling now to know that she could do this to Nathan. His breathing hadn't changed, she knew he was still asleep, but he was fully erect now and she let her palm gently cup and hold him while with her other hand she caressed him with her fingers. She marvelled at how warm and hard and silky he felt in her hands.

She felt her breathing quicken. She watched him responding to her hands, watched the smooth glide of her fingers up and down the thickened shaft, then, unable to resist, she bent her head and gently touched him with her tongue then sucked the tip of him into her mouth and let her tongue flick along the tiny ridge of skin on the underside of the head.

It was a tender, secret movement but Nathan reacted as if she'd struck him. He woke with a start then jack-knifed at the waist, jerking himself out of her mouth at the same time as he propelled her up and away from the bed. 'What the hell are you doing?'

'I thought you'd like it.' She snatched back her hand. 'After tonight, I felt like I should do something in return.' As an excuse, it was pathetic, she knew. Nothing she'd done had been for him. Stricken with embarrassment then, she reacted defensively. 'Most men love that.'

She knew milliseconds after the words were out that that was the wrong thing to say. His expression switched immediately from confusion to anger.

'I don't like it, all right?' he said strongly. 'Not now. Not from you. Not like…' He gestured around the room. 'Not like this. Get out of here, Tessa.' He hauled a sheet off the bed and thrust it at her. 'Cover yourself. You're shivering. Go back to bed and go to sleep. Now.'

She was shivering from nerves, not from cold, but she took the sheet and miserably gathered it around her body. She took a stumbling step back, and then another, horror slowly taking over from embarrassment as she realised what had happened. 'Oh, my God. We weren't making love earlier.' She stared at him blindly. 'It really was only a massage. You weren't trying to seduce me, you were trying to help me!'

'It's not that simple. Go to bed.'

But she knew that it was simple. It was all very simple and now she saw it clearly. 'You felt sorry for me.' She was mortified, but as the words came out, the reasons for everything became completely clear to her. 'You've done so much else for me, you thought, why not this too? Why not teach poor Tessa what she's been missing out on? It's all about Simon again for you, isn't it? It's still all about making up for introducing me to him because you feel guilty about him leaving.'

'I don't feel sorry for you.'

'Then why else?' she demanded, taking another step back. She held the sheet like a shroud, so high to her face that it muffled her voice. 'If you didn't want – that,' she let her eyes drop to the physical evidence of his desire, 'if that's not what you wanted from me, then why propose? And why bother with what you did for me tonight?'

'It's not pity.' But he looked confused again. 'Tessa, I do want you…'

'So much that you're throwing me out of the bedroom,' she reminded him painfully, moving as quickly as she could without stumbling again on the sheet. 'Do me a favour, Nathan. Next time you feel an urgent need to appease your conscience, try giving a bundle of cash to Greenpeace. I don't need your charity.'

chapter eleven

Nathan didn't expect to see Tessa the next morning at breakfast but she was there. Fully dressed, like he was, and freshly showered judging by the dampness of her hair but she looked pale and strained and her eyes were rimmed with red and he guessed she'd had as little sleep as he had after she'd left him. He suppressed his guilt by telling himself that he'd done the right thing. Half of it, at least. To do the absolute right thing, he shouldn't have gone near her.

She'd made scrambled eggs and grilled tomatoes and toast for him and her expression when she saw him was mingled defiance and defensiveness and he knew she expected him to argue about her cooking for him but he didn't have the heart. He took the heated plate she held out and thanked her. He had no appetite but he made an effort to appear appreciative by starting to eat.

Tessa wasn't bothering, he noticed. She'd made herself the same breakfast but she didn't touch it. 'I've decided that I'm going to go back to work on Monday,' she said stiltedly, after a little while, avoiding his eyes when he looked up sharply. 'I can't put it off any longer. I've already had two weeks more than I intended. It'll be awful not being with Thomas all the time but I don't have any choice. I won't be able to do any on call work yet overnight but I can certainly work three days a week until he's six months.'

'Not yet.' He was shocked. 'It's too early. You're still up at least two and sometimes three times every night.

You're not ready to be on your feet all day as well.'

'That's not your decision to make,' she countered. 'I'm going to speak to medical staffing and Mr Austin and Mr Barnes and the crèche today to organise everything.'

He put down his knife and fork. 'If this is anything to do with last night…'

'I decided before the weekend.' She still wouldn't look at him. 'I didn't say anything because I knew you'd try and talk me out of it and I didn't want to spend all this week arguing about it. And it doesn't matter what you think because it's nothing to do with you.'

Against his will, he was forced to acknowledge that, technically, at this time, that was true. But knowing that didn't make him any happier with the situation.

Peter Austin arrived on the main Gynaecology ward at nine-thirty. Nathan and Honour were already waiting. He beamed at them. 'Tessa called me this morning to say she's coming back next week,' he told them. 'That's good news.'

'Only three days a week to start,' warned Nathan.

'Monday, Tuesday and Friday,' the older man confirmed. 'She'll come back to full time after the next registrar changeover. What do you think?'

'They're probably the best choices,' Nathan agreed stonily. He knew Tessa had chosen the days not because they were convenient for her but because they were the three busiest ones for the team, clinic and theatre wise.

'No news from the father then?'

Nathan shrugged. As far as he knew Simon had made no attempt to contact Tessa but then she wouldn't necessarily tell him if he had.

'Bad business.' The consultant shook his head. 'The man needs a good kick in the pants.'

After touring the wards, with Nathan reminding his boss of their patients and their problems, introducing him to those he hadn't met yet and updating him on their investigations and progress since his last ward round, they finished in the Delivery Suite.

'Mr Austin!' Claire Davies winked and grinned at Nathan when they walked in through the main doors. 'We haven't seen you in ages. Both you and Mr Barnes have been a bit scarce. Keeping you busy in private are they?'

'Busy enough,' Nathan's consultant agreed happily. 'Busy enough, Claire. As usual. Er…Nathan?'

'Only one of ours here at the moment,' Nathan told him, scanning the white-board quickly to be sure there'd been no admissions in the hour since he'd last visited. 'Lucy Stone in room four is progressing well and I don't anticipate any problems. Claire?'

'She's fine,' the midwife confirmed. 'Her baby won't be long now.'

'Sounds as if you both have things under control as usual.' Peter Austin nodded and consulted his watch. 'There's no need for me to disturb these mothers. If there's anything you need from me during the day, Nathan, I'll be in my rooms. Goodbye, Claire.'

'Bye, Mr Austin,' the midwife chimed. When the doors swung shut after the obstetrician she turned back to Nathan. 'The others were saying Tessa's back Monday. True?'

'That's what she's planning.'

'Great! We've missed her smiling face round here. And you'll be happy to have her back of course.'

'It's too soon for her to be starting work again.'

'But at least you'll be able to keep your eyes on her here,' Claire said breezily. 'You'll be able to make sure she doesn't tire herself out. You won't be having to ring her up five times a day to make sure she hasn't been silly enough to fall in the pool, or if she's forgotten to eat enough vitamins, or, heaven forbid, sign a lease without your permission.'

Nathan eyed her heavily. 'Claire?'

'Yes, Nathan?'

'Shut up.'

'I love it when you give me orders,' she said softly. 'It sends me all goose-bumpy.' But she smiled. 'Just don't forget I've worked you out, you fraud.'

Nathan could only hope that Tessa never found him that transparent.

Tessa spent the whole of Wednesday in a mental fog. She did all the things she was supposed to do, she played with Thomas and looked after him and took him with her to look at a house an estate agent had rung her about and then they stopped at the Botanical Gardens on the way back for a walk. She spent two hours in the afternoon in Nathan's garden, working on the raised beds she was creating overlooking the pool, and when the sun moved off the washing line she brought in the washing and the sheets that Nathan must have hung there before he'd gone to work. But all the time her brain was stuck back on the night before. Not on the humiliating part, in the other bedroom, that was too awful to contemplate, but on the astounding part.

She'd never thought she was missing out on anything before. She'd dismissed the mindless, ecstatic contortions of women in movies and in magazines and books as exaggerated and ludicrous, designed only to titillate the idiot men who watched them. She'd copied those women, because men so plainly expected that, but her brain had always stayed cynically aloof. Even with Simon, she was painfully aware, she'd been secretly contemptuous that men could be so easily deceived.

Now she knew that she was the ludicrous one. She was the one deserving of contempt because she'd been pathetic. It wasn't surprising at all that she'd been able to fool them because probably most of the women they touched really did moan and beg and writhe and arch their backs in exactly the same way she always had only they did it in genuine passion.

She understood the phsycology of orgasm. If she'd expected anything, it had been a little thrill throughout her body. That alone had been hard enough to imagine. She could never have envisaged anything as heated or desperate as the way she'd felt when Nathan had touched her. Nor anything as devastating as the wave after wave of pleasure that had finally swept her whole body, leaving her a quivering, exhausted wreck.

As she pushed Thomas' stroller around the gardens and then later at the supermarket and on the drive back up into Khandallah, she found herself looking at women everywhere. Old women carrying shopping bags and getting on and off buses, young women jogging through the gardens, students with spiky hair and pierced eyebrows, women with babies and tired women manning the checkout counters, she studied them all, stared at them, tried to read behind their faces. How was it? she wondered bemusedly, how was it that they could look so normal and so calm and unflustered when probably most of them had been having orgasms all their adult lives?

By around the time Nathan was due home from work she had Thomas fed and in bed and on the off chance that Nathan would be home to eat, she'd prepared a special meal.

She'd bought fillet steak and she'd baked potatoes in layered slices with herbs and a dash of cream, a dish he'd complimented her on the only other time he'd been home to eat it when she'd made it for him. To go with those she'd prepared a big, crunchy salad containing lots of fresh rocket and peppers and roasted baby tomatoes.

Seconds after she saw the Audi swing around into the carport, his door opening sent a shimmer of reflected sunlight across the pool to the house. She wiped her nervous hands on a towel, took a chilled bottle of beer out of the fridge and opened it.

She registered the lines around his eyes and mouth as he walked in and guessed work had been demanding. 'Busy day?'

'Frantic. What's this?' He looked at the beer. 'Trying to obliterate a few memories?'

She felt herself colour at that. 'I opened it for you.' She searched for some sign that he'd had as much trouble getting last night out of his head as she had, but Nathan merely studied her dispassionately for a few seconds before taking a long mouthful of his drink.

He was used to it, she thought sickly. He was completely used to women falling apart in his arms. No doubt it had happened to him hundreds of times. He had no idea how much it had affected her and it hadn't been remotely special to him.

'How's Thomas?'

'Tired. He's just gone down. Are you going out?'

'Not tonight.'

'Then dinner's almost ready if you want to change.' He didn't want to talk about it, she realised. He was still angry about her waking him the way she had and he wanted to forget the whole sorry episode. She felt cold. 'All I have to do is grill the steaks.'

'Steak?' He raised his brows at her as he took another mouthful of his beer on his way through the kitchen. 'You don't like steak and you shouldn't have gone to any trouble for me.'

'It's never any trouble.' It seemed bizarre to her that a little thing like cooking a meal for him, something she enjoyed so much, should irritate him the way it did. For her, being able to do something nice for him was a rare treat. In all the time they'd been staying she'd barely had a chance to cook. And he didn't like puddings so even on the occasional nights he ate at the house she hadn't had a single chance to show off. Her most fantastic recipes were all for desserts and her chocolate mousse was out of this world.

He returned, in casual pants, a white T-shirt and a loose fitting, olive V-neck jumper now instead of his work clothes, as she was preparing to serve the steaks. He'd left his feet bare. 'Where did Thomas get the little kea he's holding?'

'Your mum dropped it in at the weekend.' Her voice still sounded self-conscious and muted. Nathan's parents often called to see Thomas but Nathan's mother had visited on Saturday – Nathan had been at work – on her own on her way down to have lunch in Wellington with Zoe. 'He loves it. And his posh new pyjamas are from Zoe,' she added. Nathan's sister had visited her the week before. 'She bought him a little jacket as well for winter. It's absolutely beautiful.'

Nathan's family had been very welcoming. She'd worried at first that they might think her impolite for the way she and Thomas were imposing on Nathan the way they were, but instead they'd been treating her almost like one of their own. She'd talked to his mother and explained that there was nothing going on, to clear the air, but that hadn't changed anything and they were all still very nice to her. 'I wish Zoe wouldn't spend so much on him. I'm sure she can't afford to be so extravagant.'

'She's a generous soul.' Nathan thanked her for the meal she passed him. 'Brain like a rabbit but her heart's always been in the right place. Don't say anything to her about the money because you'll embarrass her. This looks incredible.'

Tessa gave him a distracted smile. 'Zoe's brain can't be too rabbit-like,' she offered. Although the younger doctor did often seem…fey, she obviously didn't lack intelligence. 'She did well at Med school. Straight As, your mother told me.'

'A source of mystery to us all,' he revealed with what Tessa decided must be typical brotherly candour.

Over the meal the discussion stayed benign and to keep him happy she did her best to keep it that way. Carefully skirting around any issues that might be too personal, they discussed Thomas and work and then Zoe and Jack. Nathan's brother was due back in New Zealand to give a talk at a medical conference in Auckland and while he was in the country he was planning a flying visit to his parents and to Nathan. 'Dad told him you mentioned that the Paeds department is looking for funding to appoint a new consultant at the end of the year,' Nathan explained. 'I suspect he wants to check out the place. He'll stay here a couple of nights if that's all right with you.'

Tessa looked at him blankly. 'Of course it's all right with me.' She was bemused he thought he needed to consider her. 'It's your house. Besides, Thomas and I will have moved out by the weekend. I'm starting work on Monday so I need somewhere to live immediately. I've found somewhere I like. It's in Berhampore and I've had a look today from the outside and it looks nice. It's vacant and the landlord's painted the inside and it's all ready for tenants. The only view is of the street unfortunately and the garden's a bit neglected but it's near a park and there's a big lawn and the house is comfortable. I've watched you inspecting places often enough to know what to look for myself now so you won't need to see it. The agent's going to show me around the inside first thing Friday morning. If the owners are happy with my details, I should be able to sign a lease straight away.'

But instead of the relief she was expecting, Nathan looked impatient. 'Yes, I have to see it. I'm not on call this weekend so I'll look at it on Saturday after my ward round. Don't sign anything until I've had a chance to check it out. Better still, don't sign one at all. I've told you, you don't have to leave.'

'Yes, we have to leave.' They'd finished eating now and she gathered up their plates and the leftover salad then carried everything over to the bench beside the dishwasher. 'Now more than ever. We can't stay forever. Much as I appreciate everything you've done for us, sooner or later...'

'There's no sooner or later,' he interrupted. 'And what does "now more than ever" mean?'

'Now that I'm going back to work,' she said strongly, although that hadn't been what she meant and she knew from his scathing look that he wasn't deceived. 'I need to be independent again. Thomas and I need our own home.'

He pushed back his chair. 'Because of last night.'

'Not solely.' But Tessa felt hot colour crawl up from her

neck to cover her face. 'But it's obvious to both of us, I'm sure, that that adds to the urgency of the situation, yes.' She tightened her chin and collected her nerves. 'This meal was supposed to be a way of apologising to you about this morning. I shouldn't have...have done what I did. I made assumptions even though you warned me once not to and I'm sorry. I misunderstood but I don't want you to think that I'm not appreciative of everything you did for me last night.'

'Appreciative?' He ran a hand though his hair. He looked tired again and under stress and she felt bad that she was contributing to that. 'Don't keep using that word. I didn't touch you because I wanted your appreciation. And stop apologising. And don't leave. I don't want you to leave.'

'We have to.' Her voice was stilted. She walked to the window and stared out at the pool. In the reflection, she saw him watching her. 'I can't bear it,' she said. 'I can't bear knowing that you're trying to make up for Simon all the time. It makes me ill to think that you feel sorry for me.'

'You're mad.' He swore under his breath then strode towards her and then his hands at her hips jerked her back hard against him so her head touched his chest below his chin and she was immediately and dizzyingly aware of his arousal. Does this feel like I feel sorry for you?' he demanded, his voice raw. 'I didn't push you away this morning because I didn't like it. If I thought for one second that you knew what you were doing I wouldn't be able to keep my hands off you.'

Tessa tipped her head back against him, her eyes closing. Right then, with her insides feeling as if they were beginning to melt again against him, she could almost think he believed what he was saying. His hands lifted slowly and when his thumbs slid across her nipples she trembled in response. 'If you liked it, then why…'

'Because you don't owe me anything. I know you, I know how your crazy brain works. That's what you were thinking.'

'Only a little,' she admitted. 'I know I said that but mostly I wanted to do it for myself.'

He made a rough sound in his throat then pressed his mouth hard to her head. 'This would be a hell of a lot easier if you were normal.'

'I'll never be that.' The words came out as a wretched sigh. 'I don't think I'll ever be normal. Not in my entire life.'

'I didn't mean you so much as the situation.' His arms tightened around her hips. 'After last night, you have to realise there's nothing wrong with you. I don't know what's gone on in the past but I do know there's never been anything wrong with the way you respond. If you trust yourself or your partner enough to be aroused, it doesn't take any special skill to tip you all the way. All that's been wrong in the past is that you've probably never felt secure enough before to be able to let go.'

'Oh and I really feel secure now,' she said brokenly. 'As if.'

'Why not?' He bit softly at the lobe of her ear, making her shiver. 'I'm not going anywhere.'

'I'll sleep with you if you want. I won't marry you, that's silly, but I will sleep with you.'

'*What*?'

'We can have sex if you still want to.' It was almost a whisper. Tessa turned around slowly. She felt the colour drain out of her skin, but she met his burning gaze head on. 'For however long you want. And then we'll do our best to go back to the way we were before. It'll be hard, I know, I've never tried being friends with anyone afterwards before, but then I've never been friends with anyone else before becoming lovers either, so perhaps it will work. And if it doesn't – then we're no worse off than we are now. We can't seem to spend more than five minutes together any more without arguing.'

'Are you offering this for me or for you?'

'For both of us, I hope.'

'You won't marry me, but you'll have an affair with me? Even though that's the one thing you've been fighting against this whole time. Why? Because you're *curious* now?'

'Of course I'm curious.' The comment should have been wry, amused even, to deflect his probing, she knew that. But it came out quiet and earnest. 'I know in my heart that it's not going to work with us and that that's going to be hard to cope with, but I don't think I can walk away now. I want to touch you. I want to do to you what you did to me.'

'So it's either a pay back or an experiment. Too bad.' His mouth looked hard and he took a step back away from her. 'I don't like you paying back and I'm not a lab rat. If you want me, you'll have to marry me. Then you can touch all you want.'

She shook her head. 'I've already said I can't…'

'Yeah. I remember.' He walked away. 'Let me know when you change your mind. I'll be in the study. I need to do a few hours' research for work on line. Thanks for dinner but next time it's my turn to cook for both of us. Leave the dishes where they are and I'll fill the machine when I'm finished.'

'You can't walk out on me,' she cried after him. 'You started this. I would have been perfectly fine if you hadn't done what you did.'

'If you're frustrated you know what to do.'

'And what's that? Beg?'

He stopped at the door and turned back slowly. 'Tessa, I didn't do anything for you last night that you can't do for yourself.'

chapter twelve

Tessa stared at him blankly at first but then slowly she felt the colour flood back into her face and her throat. 'You're saying I should learn how to do...*that*?' His steady look only amplified her horror. 'I've tried it before,' she said shrilly. 'The olive oil, remember? And I told you, it didn't work. Filing my nails is more exciting than that and, by the way, a whole lot more fun.'

'Take off your clothes and turn off a few lights and take your time. If you're still having trouble in a couple of hours when I've finished in the study, I'll give you some hints.'

Tessa drew herself up stiffly and collected her dignity together like the shrouds of a ragged mop. 'I'd rather run naked up Dixon Street than waste a minute of my time trying to do that, thank you all the same.'

'Your call.' He was casual but his grin was disconcertingly knowing. 'Exercise helps. Try a swim.'

Tessa tried television. But channel after channel was showing romance or sex in one form or another and she turned off the set in disgust. 'They shouldn't be able to screen things like that,' she told Thomas. 'Not when there could be little babies watching.'

Hoping he'd distract her, she'd brought him into the living room for his feed, intending to read to him for a little while afterwards but by the time he'd finished he was dozing and it was obvious he wanted to go back to bed.

She put him down and watched while he drifted off to sleep then she prowled about the house, picking up and equally quickly dismissing various books and journals and compact discs. Thinking a bath might ease her restlessness, she took a long one then brushed her teeth and changed into a nightie but she was still wide awake. Stacking the dishes into the machine and sorting the day's washing didn't occupy her for long. Nathan hated her ironing for him and since he only ever pressed the absolute essentials for himself she took his sheets and pillow cases directly into his room without bothering with an iron first.

Everything smelt so fresh and clean, she couldn't resist lying face down on the newly-made bed. The oil from her massage hadn't left any marks in the cream linen, she saw. Thankfully. Rolling over, she gathered one of his pillows to her chest and lowered her head into it. She had enough to feel guilty about without having to worry about his sheets as well.

Time stretched out. She found herself not moving. She didn't think that was part of a deliberate plan, she suspected more that she was simply waiting to see what happened.

She was quite awake. She heard the door to the study open and then she heard sounds in the kitchen as if he was having a drink. The second door to his bathroom slid open and then the shower went on.

Eventually there was silence and when she opened her eyes he was standing in the doorway between his bathroom and the bedroom, a towel around his hips, watching her silently. She steeled herself but he simply said, 'I'll get Thomas' intercom.'

She'd left the window open and the curtains billowed gently in the breeze, swishing against the wall and she lay listening to them until he came back. He closed the door and put the intercom on the floor beside the bed, then lifted the sheet and came into the bed behind her. Warm hands slid up under her nightie and lifted it and Tessa sat up obediently and held her arms in the air so he could take it off over her head. Then one arm came around to cup her left breast and he hooked a leg over both of hers and pulled her back into his body.

He kissed the top of her head. 'Sleepy?'

'No.' Her voice sounded hoarse and she shook her head. 'Not really.' Not remotely. 'Did you finish your research?'

'I had trouble concentrating.' His hand gently caressed her breast and rubbed softly against her nipple and she bit her lip and arched back against him. He murmured for her to be still and to relax and he stopped the caress and moved his hand to her midriff and held her there and told her to sleep.

She tried to turn but he didn't let her and when she reached her hand around, intent on exploring the hardness she felt against her buttocks, he captured her wrists in his hand and tightened his leg against hers and held her fast. 'Be still,' he growled. 'Shush.'

She wouldn't have believed that she could sleep like that, not in the state she was in, but she must have because when the intercom relaying the sound of Thomas crying brought her back to consciousness, her breasts were sore and swollen and the clock radio by the bed told her it was almost two. Nathan was fast asleep behind her and she tried to lift his arm gently enough not to wake him, but he stiffened immediately.

He lifted his head and kissed the back of her neck. 'Thomas?'

'I have to feed him,' she whispered, disentangling her legs.

He started to come with her. 'I'll make tea.'

'No, don't.' She often made herself tea to drink while she was up at night and sometimes when Nathan was out late or still awake he'd bring her a fresh pot. 'Please. I'll feel terrible. You have to work tomorrow. Go back to sleep.'

He seemed reluctant but he must have seen that she was determined because he didn't follow her and when she came back he was sleeping again. He'd moved over to where she'd been lying and he'd buried his face in her pillow. Tessa slid into bed behind him. She put her arm around his firm tummy and kissed his shoulder and lowered her head into his back and he stirred slightly again and shifted an arm to rest it on her hip.

She lay for a little while in wonder. Nothing had happened. They hadn't kissed, they'd barely even touched, all he'd done was hold her while she slept yet she'd never felt so close to another human being.

The next time she woke it was light. They'd shifted in the night again and they were facing each other and he smiled at her and she smiled back tentatively and very slowly, his hand at her shoulder, he rolled her over on to her back and came after her. He slid one leg between hers and covered her mouth with his. Tessa went dizzy. She gripped his shoulders and dug in her fingers, opening her mouth, hungry for the taste of him, but he resisted the urgency of her response and his kiss was tender rather than passionate. Instead of staying at her mouth and deepening the embrace, he switched to her chin then her cheek and then her throat.

'It's almost seven-thirty,' he murmured, against her ear. 'I'm very, very late.' He kissed her breast. 'I have to go.'

'No. Not yet.' She lifted her head and twisted, trying to

reach his mouth but his hands at her hips held her still and he kept up the small, teasing kisses and slid down her body. Her other breast now and then her tummy button and then her hips and her thighs and then – sending her rigid – he opened her legs.

It was a caress Tessa had always hated, one that felt so painfully intimate and intrusive that she'd always gone out of her way to either discourage it or fight it off, but when Nathan's mouth touched her, she turned breathless. His tongue slowly sought out then circled her and she shuddered and tipped her head back into the bedding. Her pelvis arched and she grabbed handfuls of his hair and instead of thrusting him away she found herself holding him against her.

Nathan touched her again, very lightly, then swore softly and lifted his head. 'Big mistake when I'm running this late,' he said huskily. She saw dark colour tracking across his cheeks. 'Big, big mistake.'

He lifted himself away and she groaned a protest and came up on to her elbows. 'Nathan?'

'Not now.' He went into the bathroom and closed the door and she heard the shower turn on but when he emerged five minutes later to dress his skin was covered in goose bumps and she flushed as she guessed that he'd used only the cold tap. She lay back and watched him moving about the room, revelling in the precious intimacy of being able to study him like this.

With spare, efficient movements he quickly dressed and threw clothes and toiletries into his overnight bag. Forlornly she remembered that he was on call for the night. When he'd finished fastening his shirt buttons, he came to the bed, put his hands either side of her hips and kissed her hard. 'This day and this night are going to be hell. Every second of every minute, I am going to be thinking of you like this and wanting to be here with you. I'll say goodbye to Thomas and then I'm going. See you tomorrow night. Bye.'

'Bye.' Tessa rolled off the bed and came after him. 'I'm sorry I didn't make you breakfast.'

The look he sent her was heated enough to make her colour again. 'I liked the taste I had,' he reminded her softly, propelling her ahead of him after he'd seen Thomas to the front door. 'Pity I didn't have time to enjoy it properly. We'll save that treat for next time, hmm?' He held her against the door briefly and kissed her mouth, then her breasts, then he bent and lifted her and kissed her hip. 'On Saturday we'll stay in bed till noon.'

Tessa stared after him when he left, her heart pounding. She wondered whether that counted as a promise.

Nathan's morning was busy and arriving late didn't help. His theatre list was full and the registrar on call for gynae overnight had added three emergencies to the end of the list plus Delivery Suite was full until mid afternoon.

'At least with Tessa back three days next week you'll get some peace now and then,' one of the midwives said cheerfully when she had to call him back for the second time in half an hour in the afternoon.

Nathan grimaced. Having an extra registrar would mean that whoever was on call for the day for deliveries could concentrate on obstetrics without having to maintain gynaecology responsibilities as well but he'd still prefer Tessa spent longer on leave.

She still looked tired to him and even without other complications this week she hadn't been getting a lot of sleep. It wouldn't be difficult for her to express milk into a bottle and if he'd thought she'd accept the idea he'd have offered to get up to Thomas once a night himself. But the one time he'd raised the possibility she'd reacted as if he was insane.

'I expect she's looking forward to Simon coming back.'

Nathan looked at her blankly. 'Hmm?'

'Simon,' the midwife repeated. 'Simon Morrison. I said I expect Tessa's looking forward to him coming back next week.'

'*What?*'

'Well, everyone's saying it's true.' She seemed puzzled by his shock. 'He rang Prof Miller yesterday to see if he could get back on to the GP training scheme. He's due to fly in from Bangkok on Thursday and he wanted to be able to go straight into a job.'

Nathan stared at her. He couldn't think of a single thing to say.

Tessa was feeding Thomas just after four-thirty when she heard the Audi. She heard Nathan come inside and go into his room and shortly after he came out again she heard him dive into the pool. Her door had been closed and she guessed he'd assumed she was napping.

She finished with Thomas and quietly took him into his own room and put him down. As soon as he was asleep, she undressed and collected a towel and walked outside.

Ultimately, she was going to be hurt. She knew that. But she had no choice. She couldn't go on like this, he was all she could think about. She was going to have to deal with the consequences when she had to.

'Hello.'

Nathan, in the middle of a length, swam to the end of the pool then turned around, treading water as he looked up at her. 'Hi.'

The muscles in his chest and shoulders were wet and

sleek and Tessa swallowed heavily, shed her towel then dived in. She swam under water then came up in front of him. 'I wasn't expecting you. I thought you were on call?'

'One of the others is covering me for a couple of hours but I have to be back by six. You're not usually this brazen.' His narrowed green eyes flickered from her nude body beneath the water to the low timber fence at the boundary a few meters from the opposite side of the pool. 'Or is this for Mr Benson's benefit as well as mine? He usually comes out to water his plants around now.'

'He's in Christchurch.' Nathan's neighbours on the left side had an adult son in Christchurch, in New Zealand's South Island, and a daughter and son-in-law in Gisborne, on the North Island's East Coast. 'They're away for two weeks. We're feeding Fluffy and collecting the mail.'

'So you think you're safe, do you?'

'Who wants to be safe?' Her smile deliberately taunting, she wrapped her arms around his neck and let her body float against his. 'That feels nice,' she murmured, entwining her legs around his thighs. 'Mmm.' He was wearing shorts and gloriously through the fabric she could feel him hard against her. 'Six. That's at least an hour before you have to leave again.' She stretched herself against him. 'I like this.'

'What about this? Do you like this?' Before she could work out what he was going to do, he pressed down on her head lifted her away from him and dumped her under the water.

Tessa came up spluttering and indignant. She slicked her soaking hair back off her face then went after him and for a while they played like that together, adults playing childish games, she pursuing him determinedly and Nathan fending her off effortlessly whenever she came too close.

But it was unfair because he was so much fitter than she was that when he'd rendered her breathless and weak he was still barely breathing hard. 'This isn't how this was supposed to work,' she complained eventually, subsiding against the edge of the pool, her arms spread along the sides but her body low enough that her breasts were still concealed by the water. 'You were supposed to be so overwhelmed you hauled me right out of the pool and made love to me over there on the lounger.'

Nathan laughed. 'It wouldn't stand the stress.' He swam to her and kissed her forehead. 'And I am overwhelmed,' he teased, sliding his hands from her throat, to her breasts and then slowly down her body to her hips then her thighs. 'But you know the rules. This morning doesn't change anything. It's still no sex without the diamond. Anyway, I'd want more than an hour to make it good for you.'

'I don't know.' Dreamily, Tessa pressed her fingers to his mouth. 'The way I feel right now, five minutes might be enough. How about it?'

'No way, sweetheart.' He kissed her fingers then her forehead again. 'I'm not ever rushing you.'

'Please. Rush me.' She closed her eyes in silent delight as he pressed little kisses to her eyelashes. 'Mmm. Don't stop.'

But he did and when she blinked her eyes open in protest she saw that he'd stopped smiling now. 'I'm here because I need to tell you something.'

He was so serious she sobered in a hurry. 'What?' she whispered. What was he going to say? That he didn't want her any more? That he'd decided he did truly love

Georgette after all? Or that there was definitely someone else? '*What?*'

'It's Simon.' Nathan's eyes met hers and for a brief moment neither of them spoke, but then he said, 'I get the feeling you don't know he's coming back next week.'

'*What?*' Tessa almost sank beneath the water then but she gripped on to the side of the pool to catch herself in time. '*Are you sure*? When?'

'Thursday. He's spoken to Doug Miller and applied to come back on to the General Practice rotation. I checked with Doug an hour ago and he said he's offered him a casualty officer job for three months in town.'

Tessa stared at him. 'But he hasn't called. And what about his travelling? He hasn't been to Europe yet. As far as I know he's still in Thailand and he wanted to go from there to London. He was thinking he'd be away a few years. He wanted to see the whole world.'

'Perhaps he finally realised what he was giving up,' Nathan said heavily. 'Which doesn't mean you have to take him back. If that's not what you want then stay here. Nothing has to change. I'll deal with Simon. You don't need him.'

'Oh, that's kind but I can't stay.' Tessa's shook her head vaguely. 'That wouldn't be right. But...I still don't know.' She tried to think but she couldn't get her brain to work properly. 'Simon's Thomas' father. I can't not...' She broke off, unsure. 'I have to think.'

Her head spinning still, this time with shock, not desire, she released her arms from the sides of the pool and swam around and past Nathan, used the ladder to climb out, then quickly wrapped her towel around her shivering body and went into the house.

Nathan watched her go, then leaned his head against the

back wall of the pool. There were times, he reflected grimly, when doing the right thing felt a lot like taking a hacksaw to his own insides.

Gritting his teeth he hauled himself out of the pool, towelled himself roughly dry then went inside to get dress.

He wasn't supposed to be working Friday night or the weekend but the Karori medical staffing officer bleeped him within five minutes of him arriving back in the hospital to tell him that the Wellington doctor who was supposed to do the next day was sick and wouldn't make it.

'Also, the locum we've been trying to get for the weekend isn't going to be available. So I'm putting you down to cover from now until five Monday night,' the administrator told him. 'That's all right, isn't it?'

'Aside from being illegal,' Nathan pointed out coldly, 'yes I suppose it is.' It would mean a shift of more than a hundred hours but he'd done it before and he had no choice. Even if he objected, there wasn't anyone else to cover – the other Obs and Gynae registrar at Karori had made plans to go away for the weekend – and he could hardly walk out and leave the department without registrar supervision.

'Things will improve after next week,' the officer said brightly. 'Tessa coming back will help relieve some of the pressure on you all.'

'Not with the on call,' Nathan reminded her. 'We're still waiting on the locum you promised for that.'

'Oh no need for a locum. We've managed to twist Dr Webster's arm into covering one night a week from now on,' the voice chirped. 'She'll be doing every Tuesday.'

'*Are you mad?*' Nathan felt like strangling her. 'Her baby is nine weeks old. She shouldn't even be working days yet, let alone nights.'

'She said something about finding a babysitter,' the woman answered, evidently unconcerned about the pressure she must have exerted to get Tessa to agree to leave Thomas one entire night a week. 'Or perhaps the father's going to mind the baby, I don't know. Dr Morrison will be back by then, won't he? Whatever, it's all sorted.'

Not with him. Nathan put the phone down on the administrator and rang the house immediately but Tessa didn't answer. He left a message on the machine warning her that he wouldn't be home the next day or all weekend and asking her to get back to him urgently but she didn't call and then the night got busy and he didn't get another chance to ring her until Friday morning. Again she didn't pick up and he left another message asking her to call him, but she never did and since she seemed to be out every time he got a chance to try her over the weekend, the next time he saw her was on Monday morning when she walked into the nursing station on their main Gynae ward in time for his eight o'clock ward round.

'Tessa!' The nurses, obviously thrilled, took turns to hug her and exclaim over her. 'We were looking forward to having you here today,' the charge nurse told her happily. 'Welcome back to the madhouse!'

'Thanks.' Tessa, Nathan saw, seemed a little overwhelmed by the enthusiasm of the greetings. She looked at him nervously before turning back to the nurses. 'I almost didn't make it,' she confessed. 'I nearly lost my nerve in the crèche. Poor Thomas seems happy enough with all the fuss the girls down there were making of him but it just about killed me to leave him there.'

'You wait till he's five and off to school,' one of the other nurses told her sagely. 'That's the biggest wrench.

That's when they're growing up. I wept buckets with every one of mine.'

Nathan showed Tessa around their patients on the Gynae wards. The two consultants they worked for functioned as a team with many shared responsibilities. In Tessa's absence he'd taken over her consultant's patients as well as his own, but now she was back she was obviously keen to take over again on the three days she'd be at the hospital.

'Didn't you get my messages?' he demanded quietly in a brief moment alone while their junior doctors were distracted checking blood results.

'I tried to ring you on Thursday night but you kept being in theatre,' she said apologetically. 'After that I didn't get any more time. I went to see the house at Berhampore on Friday morning and I signed the lease straight away.' Apparently oblivious to his shock at that she continued, brightly, although her eyes avoided his the same way they'd been doing all morning, 'They wanted someone immediately and if I hadn't signed I might have lost it. I couldn't wait for you. But I checked it out thoroughly and it's fine. I used the same removal men you organised before and they moved all my stuff on Saturday. It didn't take that long since most of it was still packed. I've been going back to feed Fluffy twice a day,' she added, referring to his neighbour's cat, 'and I'll keep doing that since you'll probably forget but you'll be pleased to know you've got the house all to yourself again.'

Nathan wasn't pleased at all. 'You didn't need to rush to move out. There was no hurry.'

She looked up at him, her blue eyes so guarded it almost hurt him to look at her. 'Simon rang me on Thursday night after you left to come back to work. He needs somewhere to stay so I had no choice about the house. There's Thomas to consider, you see. We talked for a long time. Nathan…Simon and Thomas and I, we're going to be a proper family now.'

Avoiding what he knew had to be his numb expression she gently tugged her arm free of his grip and went ahead of him down the ward.

chapter thirteen

Despite her anxieties about leaving Thomas, Tessa found herself enjoying being back at work. It was fun catching up with her patients and meeting new ones and being back in the normal adult world. After two days she was still missing the time away from Thomas of course but he seemed happy enough where he was and with the crèche in the hospital grounds, she could still pop over a dozen times a day for feeding as well as to play and cuddle him whenever she could get a free moment.

It wasn't easy working closely with Nathan. She couldn't be near him without her heart starting to thunder. She couldn't look at him and not think about what it felt like when he touched her or how it had felt to slide against him, her body naked, in the pool, and she kept remembering the determined intentness of his expression when he'd told her she could stay and that he'd deal with Simon. But the loyalty she owed Simon made her ashamed of those feelings and determined to resist them.

What every argument she could have with herself in the world boiled down to was the simple fact that Simon was Thomas' father. If he was as determined to return to New Zealand and settle down and share a stable environment with her and her son as he'd sounded when he'd called her from Bangkok, then she owed it to him and Thomas to give it her best shot.

Spending hours daydreaming about Nathan and what might have been if things could have been different was stupid and selfish.

Medical staffing had insisted she cover one night on call a week even when she was working part time. They suggested she employ a babysitter if leaving Thomas proved difficult. She managed to get out of the arrangement for the first week by promising them that the following week with Simon back there definitely wouldn't be a problem.

Meaning she was going to have to throw poor Simon in at the deep end, she reflected anxiously when Thomas called her up for the third time in the early hours of Wednesday morning. Nathan had a gift for dealing with babies, including her son, but Simon had always been awkward around young children.

'But it'll be different with you,' she promised Thomas. 'Yes it will because he's going to love learning how to look after you, my darling, because he's your daddy.'

She dressed Thomas in one of the trendy little stretch-and-grow suits Nathan's sister had bought for the drive to the airport to meet his father the next morning. Unfortunately Thomas was grizzly rather than his usual sunny self and although she'd hoped he'd sleep through the journey and awake refreshed and happy again he stayed awake most of the time and still looked grumpy when she lifted him from his capsule and hurried him towards the terminal. She hoped Simon wouldn't judge him too badly. 'Anyway he'll understand in a few days what a good baby you are,' she told Thomas comfortingly.

She was shocked when Simon walked out into the waiting area. It was almost seven months since she'd seen him and although he was so tanned his hair gleamed like white gold in contrast to his skin, he'd lost a lot of weight. He looked unhealthy and gaunt. 'You're so thin!' she exclaimed, embracing him. 'Have you been sick?'

He shrugged. 'Malaria.'

'*Malaria*? Didn't you take prevention?'

'Not after a few weeks. No one bothers much when you've been there a while.' He swung his backpack to the floor and held out his arms for Thomas and Tessa passed him to him. 'This is the sprog then, is it? Doesn't look much like me.'

'Of course he does.' Tessa smiled at Thomas' bemused look as he stared up at his father but inside she was a ball of nerves as she longed, desperately, for Simon to fall in love with Thomas as madly as she had the first time she'd seen their baby son. 'He's got your smile and your nature.'

'Your chin.'

'Well, yes.' Tessa put her fingers around her chin self-consciously. 'Mmm.'

'Agh, he's wet.' Simon withdrew the hand he'd held underneath Thomas' bottom and handed him back to her with a grimace. 'It's soaked right through. Haven't you heard of disposables?'

'Bad for the environment,' Tessa mumbled. 'I'll change him in the car.'

Simon drove. He always did when they were together. He couldn't bear her cautiousness. Simon's personality, normally easy-going and casual, transformed whenever he climbed behind the wheel of a car. She saw immediately that nothing had changed. She wanted, a few times, to remind him about Thomas and ask him to slow down but she knew that wouldn't be a good idea. His responses to her interested questions about where exactly he'd been and what he'd seen in his time away had been uncharacteristically clipped and distant and there was an edginess about him she'd never felt before. She worried that in his current mood if she objected to his driving he'd only go faster and she didn't want to provoke an argument his first day at home.

'Have you heard any more about work?' she asked, relaxing a little as they caught up to a queue of traffic on the road towards the tunnel, forcing him to break since there was no room to pass.

'I start at eight in Emergency in town on Monday.'

With a sinking heart she registered that he sounded unenthusiastic. 'Normal hours?' she asked.

'Eight-till-six, the first month at least.'

'That's handy because I'm going to be on call every Tuesday night,' she revealed, relieved he wasn't going to be working awkward shifts for at least a little while. 'You'll be able to look after Thomas overnight.'

'Me?' He spared her a shocked look. 'You want *me* to look after him? What about feeding? He must be still waking overnight isn't he?'

'I'll express milk in advance,' she explained, wishing now that she'd left the subject a few more days. 'I know how to do it and I've bought all the stuff. He's a good baby, Simon. He smiles all the time and he rarely cries. He's hardly any trouble at all.'

Simon looked sceptical. They were through the tunnel now and he signalled then pulled out, accelerating so fast that the engine of her little car roared as he overtook the car in front of them and dived back into the queue in time to avoid an oncoming rubbish truck. 'What about Nathan?' he asked impatiently, sending her a sideways look once he was back in his lane. 'Couldn't he do it?'

Tessa was still gripping the handle above her door where she'd grabbed it seconds before and she blinked at him vaguely, not understanding. 'Nathan?'

'You've been staying with him, haven't you? He must

be used to Thomas by now.'

'How do you know where we were? Did he *call* you?'

'Keep your hair on.' He flung her an irritated look. 'I didn't ask him to keep tabs on you. Not that he would have if I had. Doug Miller mentioned it when I spoke to him last week.'

She let her breath out. 'We only stayed with Nathan because he kindly offered to take us in when we were about to be kicked out of the house,' she said numbly, gripping on as he raced the car around the Basin Reserve and veered off towards Berhampore. 'And yes, he offered to look after Thomas on Tuesdays but there's no need now you're back. Thomas is your son. You don't mind looking after him one night a week, do you?'

Restoring a little of her peace of mind he did, at least, look marginally shamefaced then. 'I guess not,' he said dully, and they both jerked forward as he braked hard for the curve and the pedestrians ahead. 'It's what I'm here for after all. For once in my life to do *the right thing*.'

Tessa sent him a startled look but his expression was not encouraging and she bit her lip again, electing to keep her mouth shut apart from giving him directions to the house until he'd had more of a chance to settle in. She was worrying about nothing, she told herself. She hadn't applied any pressure, she hadn't even spoken to him. Simon had chosen to come home. He had to want this to work as much as she did.

At the house he automatically put his pack in the double bedroom at the front and then he walked around, his expression neutral, checking out the rest of the house. He came back to where she was waiting with Thomas in the kitchen. 'Not bad,' he conceded. 'Could have been worse. How much are they asking?'

She told him and he winced. 'That's more than a month on the island.' He curled a hand around her neck. 'Don't I get a hello kiss then?' he muttered. 'Your breasts look good. They're bigger. Can I see?'

'No. Not yet.' Tessa flinched away from the embrace and batted away his hand. She held Thomas tightly and ducked under Simon's arm. 'It's the breast-feeding. Simon, it's been over six months. I'm very happy you're back but I want us to get to know each other again first before we sleep together. All my things are in the little bedroom. I've bought a new bed and I found a dresser and a wardrobe in a charity shop.'

His brown eyes narrowed sharply. 'Did Nate say something to you after he called me?'

'Nathan?' She felt herself colour slightly. 'I don't think so. About what?'

'Forget it.' Simon shook his head dismissively. 'It doesn't matter.' To her relief he drew back then and shrugged. 'Whatever makes you happy with the sleeping arrangements. I don't care. I was thinking of you, I thought you'd be climbing the walls by now. I need to make phone calls, let people know I'm back in town. What's for lunch?'

'Your favourite,' she told him, relaxing when she saw that the issue she'd been almost sick with worry about, wasn't going to be a problem at all. 'There's a phone in your bedroom.'

To her relief her first Tuesday night on call seemed to go all right. Thomas slept right through and when Tessa met Simon for lunch on Wednesday he seemed quite proud of his baby-minding skills. She had high hopes for the following week but a terse call from Simon before nine that Tuesday made her heart sink.

Thomas, it seemed, was refusing to settle. 'There's nothing wrong with him,' Simon told her crossly. 'He wants you. You're going to have to come home.'

'But I can't.' Tessa was on her way to Delivery Suite and it sounded as if one of her patients might need surgery. She'd been in labour most of the day and was failing to progress. Tessa had started a course of treatment earlier to try and improve her contractions and she'd popped a scalp monitor on to the baby's head and taken blood for testing so they could monitor him closely to make sure there were no signs of compromise. But if there'd been no progress now from when she'd last examined her then it would be time for her and the mother to make a decision about what they wanted to do. 'Simon, bring Thomas in. I'll try and get away for a few minutes to quieten him.'

'Better you come home,' he argued. 'I could drag him all the way up there and then have him start crying again the minute I bring him back. You have to come home. Someone will cover you. Thomas needs you.'

Tessa felt sick. 'Give me half an hour.' She'd examine her patient again and if things were still stable otherwise on the rest of the wards she'd feel happier about leaving Honour in charge for the time it would take her to reassure Thomas.

But things weren't stable *and* the unit was expecting a new admission.

'Twenty-eight-year-old, thirty-two weeks into her second pregnancy with complications,' the midwife in charge told her urgently. 'Her GP's called for an ambulance and he'll come with her. She should be here within twenty minutes.'

'Twenty minutes.' Tessa nodded. She couldn't leave. She called Simon to warn him but he sounded at the end of his tether. 'He hasn't stopped screaming since I called,' he insisted. 'He's driving me mad. I don't care what's happening, you're going to have to come home. Get old Barnsey in to look after the place,' he ordered. 'That's what he's there for, isn't it?'

Tessa knew Mr Barnes would come if he thought she needed him but the consultant was in Wellington for the evening at a Medical School meeting which meant that by the time she'd called him and explained everything, he wouldn't reach the hospital before her patient was due to arrive. Knowing she only had one option, she called Nathan's office. He'd mentioned earlier he'd be staying late doing paperwork.

She started to explain but as soon as he heard what it was she wanted he cut her off. 'Give me two minutes.'

Tessa sagged against the desk, weak with relief. She tried to thank him but he'd already hung up.

He came to Delivery Suite and Tessa quickly detailed their expected admission. 'Honour's downstairs admitting a Gynae case,' she added. 'It's a woman with a threatened miscarriage at sixteen weeks and she's coming in for the night. I'll try and scan her tonight if I get time before she goes to sleep otherwise we'll organise it for the morning. Plus there's the mother I mentioned earlier. Her baby's OK, she's progressing well now and I think she's going to be fine. I'm sorry. Thank you so much for doing this. I won't be long.'

'Don't hurry.' He held out the door for her and his smile was sympathetic. 'Drive safely.'

Simon met her at the front door with a grim face. 'He's in the bedroom,' he pronounced. 'If you can't hear him already.'

'I could hear him from outside.' Tessa ran into the room

and gathered up her son. Thomas, his face puffy and red, had obviously been crying for ages and was clearly distraught. She checked his nappy and it was wet. She changed him then tried to feed him but he wasn't interested so she tried walking. He clung to her and she wondered around the house and outside on to the lawn, bouncing him and murmuring reassurance and after a few minutes his crying settled to jerky sobs and then he quietened and when she brought him inside he decided he wanted to feed. Afterwards he put his thumb in his mouth and went to sleep against her shoulder.

Carefully, very carefully so as not to wake him, she put him back into his cot and tucked his blanket around him.

'If you go, he'll start up again,' Simon warned, when she returned to the living room. 'Best you stay. Your boss can look after things tonight.'

'I can't.' Tessa didn't know what to do. 'Come back to the hospital and stay in my room with him and if he cries again call me and I'll come up straight away. You could wait in the doctors' mess even, you could watch TV there as easily as you can here.'

'Just tell Barnsey you can't come back.'

'It's not Mr Barnes covering me there, it's Nathan. And I have to go back. We're expecting someone who may need a Caesarean tonight.'

'Nathan won't mind doing it for you.' Simon's expression brightened. 'Good old Nate. Always reliable. He won't complain. I'll give him a call.'

'No you won't.' Tessa moved quickly to cut off the phone. 'I can't, Simon. He's done too much already. I can't ask him to do my work for me. I have to go back.'

'I'm not spending the rest of my night sitting like an idiot in your on-call room,' Simon said coldly back. 'You have to make up your mind. What comes first in your life? Your son or your job?'

'Thomas, of course,' she protested. 'But I don't have to make that choice here and he's your son too. All I'm asking for is one night a week.'

'I've worked my legs off in Emergency all day,' he argued. 'That's hard work there. I'm not fussing around in clinics and wandering about the wards telling house officers and nurses what to do. I can't be expected to sit up all night mollycoddling a baby. You've spoiled him, that's the problem. You've let him get used to you coming to him whenever he cries out and when you're not there he can't handle it.'

'He'll sleep now,' she assured him, hoping desperately that she was right. 'If he wakes again bring him up to Karori and I'll try and look after him there. OK? Please?'

But he shook his head slowly. 'This isn't working.'

Tessa hung her head, feeling sick. 'This will be the last night I do on call,' she promised. 'I'll talk to medical staffing tomorrow. I'll explain I can't do it. If they tell me I'm risking my position on the rotation then I'll have to deal with that then.'

'I mean *nothing's* working. It's more than tonight. Look, basically he's a good kid, I like him, but coming back has only made me more certain I'm not ready for this yet. I thought I could handle it, I felt I had to try at least, but it's not going to work. I feel like you're smothering me again. All this cooking and cleaning and rushing around after me drives me crazy. I need more space. There's too much I haven't done in my life yet.'

Tessa swallowed heavily. She'd been expecting something like this almost from the first day he arrived back. 'We'll talk about it tomorrow,' she whispered. 'Goodnight, Simon.' She leaned forward and pressed her mouth briefly to his cheek. 'I'm sorry.'

Her new patient had been transferred from Delivery Suite where she'd arrived for assessment to one of the maternity wards. To her relief the woman lying on the bed in a hospital gown seemed calm and her colour was normal and she smiled at Tessa when Tessa hurried in. 'Hi.'

'Hi.' Tessa lifted her hand, still breathing fast from her run from the car park. 'Ms Austin?'

'Brenda, this is Tessa Webster, the other doctor I was telling you about,' Nathan explained, looking up from the notes he'd been writing. 'Her vital signs are normal, her blood count's stable and I've scanned her and the baby is fine. She's not in labour but for the moment I believe the best course is for her to stay in hospital so we can watch things carefully.'

Tessa felt some of her tension ease. She'd automatically pictured the worst-case scenario – a haemorrhage before birth could be severe enough to cause the death of a baby and in some cases the mother as well – so she'd been concerned. But given Nathan's thorough assessment of the situation, she agreed with his conclusions. 'Thank goodness,' she said breathlessly. 'You're feeling all right then?'

'Oh, fine, doctor.' The other woman smiled again.

Outside the room, Nathan cut off Tessa's attempts to thank him again. 'How's Thomas?'

'Oh, fine.' She shook her head. 'There was nothing wrong with him. He went to sleep two minutes after I got there. Poor Simon was finding it difficult.'

'Go home and stay. I'm here now and you look like you need an early night.'

'It's stress more than tiredness.' They were walking down the shadowy corridor now towards the nursing station and she lifted one hand and rubbed at her temples with her thumb and forefinger. 'And thanks for the offer, Nathan, but I can't ask you to…'

'Yes you can. I insist.' He took her hand away and stopped her and looked closely down at her, his eyes narrowed and assessing. 'If it was up to me you wouldn't even be here tonight. You shouldn't have to do on call work yet. You're not ready for it.'

'I'm going to talk to someone tomorrow about stopping,' she admitted. 'Hopefully they won't make me leave altogether. Nate, I don't know what to do. I think Simon's thinking about going away again.'

He didn't say anything but made a soft sound and held out his arms and she went into him and let her head rest against his chest. His arms folded around her. There was nothing sexual about the embrace, just warm, solid, reassuring comfort, but still however easy it would have been to stay there with him forever, that wasn't the way life worked and eventually she had to force herself to step away before she lost the power to.

'I'll be all right,' she reassured him, not meeting his eyes. After two weeks of living with Simon again she'd come to realise, paradoxically, how much easier her life had been when he'd been away. 'It's Thomas I feel for,' she added sadly. 'And Simon, later, if he goes now, because eventually he'll realise how much he's missed not seeing Thomas grow up.'

'Go home,' Nathan ordered. 'Don't argue. I'm staying to cover you. Try and get some sleep.'

'Thank you.' Tessa felt guilty about letting him do this but she also felt overwhelming relief and she knew then that she'd never loved any man the way she loved Nathan. All the other feelings, the other relationships she'd tortured herself over for so long, had been like hiccups compared to this. It was poignant, and tragic, of course, but it was life and she'd deal with it in a little while when she was more together. 'I would like to do that,' she whispered. She had the next two days off but she was due back on the wards at the end of the week. 'I'll see you Friday.'

Medical staffing put up a fight the next morning about her refusal to commit herself to any more after-hours duties but they didn't threaten her with losing her position on the rotation so she had that, at least, to be grateful for.

Simon organised himself with a speed that left her reeling. He quit his job on Thursday and when she and Thomas came home from the hospital Friday night he brandished an air ticket to Frankfurt. 'Tomorrow morning,' he told her cheerfully. 'I'll be in Europe by Sunday. You don't mind do you?'

'Of course not.' What else could she say? At least he was looking happy again. He hadn't since he'd been home. Not from the moment he'd arrived at the airport. 'How long do you think you might be away this time?'

He shrugged. 'Who knows? A few years?'

Still feeling a bit dazed she bundled Thomas into the new car seat Simon had kindly bought him and went with him to the airport Saturday morning. She and Thomas waved him off then she drove slowly back through the city.

She stopped at a supermarket. Mallowpuffs – chocolate covered marshmallow biscuits ones with caramel on a crunchy base – were on special for the week and, in need of serious comforting, she bought a packet for lunch and afternoon tea and several packets to keep in her cupboard.

Thomas fell asleep again on the drive to the house and she carried him inside carefully, changed him and put him to bed then returned for her groceries.

Nathan was there, already lifting the bags out of the back seat where she'd left them. 'You left the door open.'

Tessa blinked up at him. 'But where'd you come from?' He'd never visited her at the house and since moving out of his home the only times she'd seen him were at Karori.

'Work.' Holding her groceries in his arms he simply returned her startled look calmly. 'I talked to Simon yesterday.'

'And he told you when he was leaving and he probably asked you to keep an eye on me so you thought you'd better call by and see how I was,' she finished for him. 'Thanks. That was a lovely thought. But as you can see we're back from the airport and I'm fine.'

She held out her hands for the bags and after a brief hesitation he passed them to her. 'You're coming back to the house.' He gestured around at her overgrown lawn with its rusted swing and tractor-tyre sandpit. 'There's too much here for you to maintain on your own. I'll pay out the lease until they find new tenants and you can come back.'

Tessa couldn't let him do it. She couldn't let him sacrifice so much for her. He had to live his own life and she had to live hers. This time, *this one time*, she was determined to be strong. She'd been wrong that day in the swimming pool to think she should grab for everything she could while she had the chance. Ultimately the least painful way for her to cope with her feelings for Nathan had to be for her to cut everything off now while she still had a fragment of strength left.

'I can manage,' she insisted quietly. 'Thomas and I are

going to be all right. Please don't worry about us.'

'So you want me to walk away and leave?' He looked irritated. 'I won't do that. I *can't* do that. I know you can manage, but I'm in your life to stay. I don't want to take over, I want to help.'

'We don't need you to help,' she insisted, gently but firmly. 'Please go away. We both know you could teach classes in how to rescue damsels in distress, and I thank you for everything you've done for us, but my life will be a whole lot easier from now on if you stay out of it and let Thomas and me fend for ourselves.'

chapter fourteen

Nathan stared at Tessa for a few tense moments but then he went up the path after her, fast, but Tessa had too much of a head start and she ran ahead of him and when she slammed her front door in his face he was forced to stop short.

He rarely lost his temper but he was close to losing it now. 'Tessa, open this door immediately.'

'Go away.' Her voice came out muffled by the timber but he decided she sounded appropriately worried.

He rattled the door handle, then scowled as the blasted thing almost came apart in his hands. It might suit his purposes for the place to be easy to break into now but thought of Tessa losing in a burglary what few possessions she had because of that ease did nothing for his sense of reasonableness.

'You've got five seconds,' he shouted. 'If you don't open this door I'm going to rip the bloody thing off its hinges.'

It wasn't a bluff, he meant it, and he started counting.

She let him get to four before opening the door an inch. 'Go away,' she hissed.

Nathan put his foot inside the door, then he wedged it the rest of the way with his shoulder. Her eyes spat blue fireworks-sparks at him and he thought she'd never looked more beautiful but still he glared back just as furiously. 'What the hell was that supposed to mean?'

'I told you.' She looked enraged. 'We do not need you rescuing us again.'

'*Rescuing*?' The accusation left him as incredulous as he was furious. 'What are you talking about?'

She backed quickly and he took that to mean she'd read his expression appropriately. 'That's what you've been doing,' she cried hoarsely. 'You're too chivalrous for your own good. It's your nature. It's the way you are and you can't help yourself.'

'You're wrong,' he said strongly.

'No, I'm not.' She shook her head at him, sending her dark curls flying. 'You don't know how easy it would be for me to let you,' she cried. 'You don't understand how easy it would be for me to let you take over and fix everything. But I can't bear it. I can't bear you feeling sorry for me. And if I let you take over again now I'll get in so deep there'll be no way out. Can't you see how humiliating that'll be for me?'

'*Humiliating*?' Nathan's heart felt as if it wanted to jump right through his chest. 'Are you insane?'

'Not yet but I will be if you don't leave right now.'

But Nathan wasn't going anywhere. Not until he'd said things he'd been wanting to say for weeks. 'If I had *rescued* you the way I wanted,' he said harshly, 'believe me, your life would be different now. I have spent six years going out of my way not to interfere in your life, regardless of how much I wanted to and how much you needed me. I can't even begin to list the numbers of times I've wanted to step in and try and shake some sense into you.'

'What are you talking about?' she demanded. 'You've done nothing but step in. When you made us move to your house…'

'You had a four-week-old baby, you were about to be evicted and you had nowhere to go. That wasn't trying to take over your life, that was being a friend.'

'You help *too* much,' she accused.

Nathan made an impatient sound. 'I'll tell you when I should have helped. I should have helped the first time you went out with Simon. I should have hauled you away from him and told you a few home truths right then and there. I wanted to warn you he'd never grow up. I wanted to warn you you'd never be able to rely on him. I wanted to tell you that it wasn't his fault, that there was nothing anyone could do about it, but that was the way things were. But I didn't. I stepped back and I let you involve yourself with him and then I watched him stuff up your life the way I always knew he would.'

'He didn't,' she railed. 'Simon gave me the most precious gift in the world.'

'He walked out when you needed him most.'

'He came back!'

'Only to get your hopes up before dumping you both so he could go racing off to Europe with some German model,' he said savagely. He regretted the words immediately he saw her pale. 'You didn't know?' he demanded hoarsely. 'He didn't tell you?'

'I don't care,' she said faintly. 'He said he had a friend in Frankfurt, someone he could stay with, but it doesn't matter who it is. I don't care what he does as long as he's happy. It's his life.'

He didn't believe her about not caring but her feelings for Simon were something he was going to have to learn to live with. 'If what I'd wanted was to rescue you, I could have done it hundreds of times. I could have done it after every one of those Auckland weekends, I could have done it when you used to run around cleaning up after him like a slave, I could have left you the first time, I could have done it in those first few days after you took Thomas home. I could have done it when I kissed you for the first time and I could have done it any time after that.' She turned away abruptly at that, her skin colouring, but he knew she knew he was right and he knew she was still listening.

'I could have done it anytime these past two weeks when you've looked at me and your hands have trembled and I've known all I had to do was reach right out and touch you and you'd dissolve in my arms. The point is, I didn't. I didn't interfere any of those times. I let you make up your own mind and go your own way.'

'Then why aren't you doing that now?' She spun around to face him again, her arms crossed like defensive shields over her chest. 'I asked you to go away but that didn't stop you forcing your way in here.'

'Because I've had enough. I've had enough going gentle with you. I've had enough holding back and letting you make your own decisions because nine times out of ten you get them wrong. This rescuing obsession of yours works both ways you know. I'm not any keener on the idea that you think of me only as someone to turn to when you're in trouble than I was before Simon turned up again. And I sure as hell don't like the idea of getting you on the rebound from him. Why do you think I didn't want to rush you into anything when you were at the house? I didn't want to touch you until I had you legally tied down enough to be sure there was no way he was going to be able to come back into our lives and take you away. But a man could go mad waiting for you to see sense and I'm not letting that happen to me. I'm not standing back and letting years go by while you work out whatever it is you think you need to work out. Simon's gone and he's not coming back. Face that, and learn to live with it. I told you'd once that eventually you'll understand you're better off without him and it's still true.'

He paused for a second then went on strongly, 'We'll take essentials in the cars tonight then call the removal firm on Monday. They should start offering us a discount about now. As soon as I can organise it we're getting married and in the meantime I'll find out how I go about adopting Thomas.'

She opened and closed her beautiful mouth a few times but nothing came out.

'I'll be a good father to him, Tessa. I already love him as if he were my own son. We're going to be happy together. We're going to have a wonderful life and we're all going to be very, very happy. If Simon ever comes back, he'll be welcome in our home as Thomas' father. But if he lays one hand on you...'

'He didn't. We didn't. Not in these two weeks. Nothing happened.'

He'd meant never to ask her that. It was something he'd intended spending the rest of his life never knowing and never wanting to know. But he felt a fierce stab of pleasure at her response.

'It was the first time I'd ever said no to him. You taught me to do that.' She sounded faint. 'Rather a big step for me, I thought. It wasn't even as hard as I thought it would be.'

'I'm glad.' The words went nowhere near describing how he felt about that but they were all he could come up with. 'But if he ever does touch you again, Tessa, I'll kill him. You might want to warn him of that when next you talk to him.'

She still didn't say anything and he decided to take that

as general agreement with everything.

Since she'd left the shopping bags sprawled across the floor just inside the door, he collected them up and carried them in the direction of where he expected he'd find the kitchen. 'This place isn't bad,' he conceded, looking around. Being in the valley where it was, rather than up on the hills, the only views were of the surrounding neighbours but it had been renovated and it was well lit and spacious and he thought she could have done worse. 'Better than I expected.'

He didn't bother unpacking all the groceries. He simply lifted out the milk and ice-cream and puddings and put them in the fridge so they wouldn't get dangerously warm before they took them to the house. He grimaced at the thick stack of chocolate biscuits she'd bought but felt marginally reassured by the fruit and vegetables in the last two bags.

He heard her sandals slip-slapping lightly against the tiles as she walked along the hall towards him. 'Is there going to be actual sex involved this time?' he heard her ask raggedly.

Nathan stilled. He waited a few minutes then turned around slowly. He studied her little toes, then lifted his eyes to the line of colour staining her cheeks. 'Yep.'

He saw her swallow. 'That's all right then. I thought I should ask.'

'I'm not doing this for that.'

'I wasn't sure.' The colour deepened now. 'I mean, I didn't think it could be that but I didn't know what otherwise it could...' She drifted off, then lifted eyes that had till then been hidden by her lashes. 'I was puzzled because you've never exactly found me impossible to resist when you've been offered the chance.'

Her response left him incredulous. 'I did what I thought was right. It wasn't easy not making love to you but I thought it was still too soon for you. In the pool that day I knew he was coming back.'

'I'm glad we didn't go all the way,' she told him hollowly. 'If we had and it had damaged things with Simon, then for Thomas' sake I'd always have wondered whether things might have been different if I hadn't been with you.'

Nathan knew that. He'd never doubted that his choice had been the right one. It hadn't helped his frustration or his peace of mind and at times he'd worried that he might not be able to keep the vow he'd made to himself, but he'd known he had no choice. His mouth compressed with remembered bitterness. 'As soon as I told you about him, you jumped straight out of the pool. You don't think it might have been polite to mention you still loved him when you were in bed with me the night before?'

'I might have if my feelings were that straightforward.' Her small chin lifted. 'But they weren't. I was confused. I didn't know how I felt and I needed time to think. I had to consider Thomas, you know that. I had to try and do the right thing for him. I love Simon. I'll always love him. He's Thomas' father. But I realised – at the airport I realised that it's not a romantic love any more. These two weeks it's been more as if I have another child around. I care about him a lot but I'm not in love with him any more. I thought, from the way you were with me, that you must have understood that before I did.'

Nathan started to wonder whether he'd understood anything. 'What are you saying?'

'What are *you* saying?'

'That now Simon's out of your life for good there's no

reason for me to hold back on what I want. That you're mine now and that when you come to me now, you should know that there's never going to be any going back for you, because I love you so much that letting you go this time almost killed me. I'm not ever going through that again.'

She went pale as if he'd hurt her. 'No you don't,' she whispered. 'You don't love me like that. You love me as a friend. Nathan, you do not have to say that…'

He swore. 'I'm not saying it to make you feel good. For God's sake, you stupid woman, I'm not that bloody self-sacrificing. You have driven me almost insane at times but I'm still here because I'm in love with you. I want to spend the rest of my life with you.'

But she still looked confused. 'You *love* me?' she echoed. '*Love* love?'

He lifted his eyes fleetingly to the ceiling. 'You're the only person who doesn't seem to realise it. I've had Claire on my back about you every day for the past month and she hasn't kept her mouth shut because ever since Simon's been back all the other midwives have been giving me these pitying looks. Tessa, you and Thomas are unbearably precious to me. I will make you happy. If life was perfect and we all got what we wanted then in return I would want love from you too. Not need or dependence or obligation or gratefulness or desire, but love. But life isn't perfect and now I'm prepared to compromise. I want you too much not to use sex if that's what it's going to take to hold you.'

'Since when? Since when have you loved me?'

He lifted one shoulder. The truth was, he didn't know exactly. Not for sure. He'd loved her for a long time as a friend but the painful, gut-wrenching wanting hadn't come until these last months. 'Is that important?'

'I've been thinking lately that I might have loved you for years,' she said faintly. 'That sounds so awful, doesn't it? Poor Simon. But I didn't know. You never gave me any encouragement you see and I didn't even start to realise until I thought you wanted Georgette. I was so jealous. I kept telling myself that I was being silly and I tried to pretend it didn't mean anything, but it was more than that. Those nights when you used to go out with Claire and the others were like torture for me. You accused me once of keeping tabs on you and I made up some excuse, but the truth was, I was. Never mind Thomas keeping me awake, it was waiting for you that kept me sitting up by his window every night you were out. I don't know what I'd have done if one night you hadn't come home. Probably I'd have sat up all night.'

Nathan sagged back against the bench behind him. He'd thought he had everything sorted out, everything sanely and sensibly sorted out for a contented existence but suddenly she was offering him paradise. 'You love me.'

She lifted up her arms, her expression bewildered as if she'd thought that had to be obvious. 'What's not to love?'

'I could give you a hundred answers, but I'd be a fool to do it.' He folded her into his arms and kissed her until she was laughing and breathless and his heart felt so full his chest hurt.

When the kisses slowed she dragged her mouth away and looked up and dimpled at him. 'Thomas is still asleep. Don't you think we'd better hurry up and make sure that you and I are completely compatible? In every way, if you know what I mean.'

Nathan thought about it. As much as he could think

about it. As much as he could think about anything right then. 'I guess that can be arranged,' he decided finally. 'Sure. No reason why not. After the wedding.'

'After the wedding?' He felt her stiffening in his arms. '*What?*'

Nathan lowered his head. 'Only way I can be sure you'll stick around,' he said roughly.

'Oh, I'm going to stick around,' she whispered, dissolving against him. 'You are not going to get rid of me easily. I promise you, Nathan my darling, Thomas and I are going to be sticking around for a very, very, very long time.'

They had a church wedding followed by a reception at the house. They and the contractor Nathan employed had to spend every hour they could spare bringing Tessa's landscaping plans to life, and the final result, with the newly-installed lighting highlighting the dramatic grasses and flaxes and exquisitely-mounded hebes surrounding the pool, looked wonderful.

Zoe, Nathan's sister and Tessa's bridesmaid, drank too much of the caterer's punch and fell over Fluffy, who'd strolled over from next door to investigate the noise and get petted, and into the pool. Tessa's bouquet, thrown backwards over her head, hit Nathan's brother Jack, his best man, in the middle of his chest where he stood at the bar. With an exasperated grimace Jack hurled the arrangement straight into the pool and that sent half a dozen female guests flying in fully dressed straight after it. After that the party shifted properly to the pool.

Nathan's parents – excited about looking after Thomas overnight – had left early with him at around midnight. When pretty much everyone but them was either in the pool or sprawled around it and looking in no hurry to leave, Tessa took her new husband by the loose ends of his bow tie and led him away.

Their cars were parked in but Jack's Porsche wasn't and since he'd been stupid enough to leave his keys in it, they stole it. The plan had been to stay at the house the night before collecting Thomas the next afternoon in plenty of time to catch their honeymoon flight to Queenstown, but no way was Tessa going to miss out on her wedding night because their guests were having too much of a good time to consider politely leaving them alone.

They checked into the bridal suite of one of the downtown hotels close to the harbour. Nathan flung open their door and lifted her into his arms and carried her past the roses and the huge basket of tropical fruit and the champagne chilling in the ice bucket and, alarmingly, the absolutely *huge* bed, to the window with its water and the light-speckled hills and star-speckled vista. He put her down in front of it all, and slid his arms around her, holding her back against him. 'Great view.'

'Beautiful.' Tessa tipped her head back as he peppered kisses along the line of her jaw to her throat. She was trembling inside. The weeks of slow, sensuous massages he'd forced her to endure before the wedding, the intimate, detailed explorations of each other's bodies, always stopping short of the ultimate embrace she craved, had left her sick with impatience and frantically anticipating this moment.

But suddenly now, now it was actually here, she started to grow nervous. Not of Nathan, or what was going to happen – she trusted him utterly – but that she might finally now, when it came to the most intimate caress of all, disappoint him. She wanted so much to please him and a little part of her began to worry that she might not be able to respond to him the way she so desperately wanted to.

'Nathan? You know if...if nothing happens the way it should tonight, with actual sex, I mean, it doesn't mean I don't trust you and love you.'

'Oh, but I'm going to take it as that,' he said casually. 'I'll be inconsolably offended.'

'You can't say things like that.' She tried to wiggle free. 'Even as a joke. That's too much pressure. Nothing will ever happen if I'm under pressure.'

Nathan smiled. 'Let's see, shall we?' Laughing at her indignant struggles he swept her up again and carried her to the bed. He dumped her on to her front then while she lay miserably protesting but too bemused to resist again he began unfastening the trail of tiny buttons holding her dress together. 'Let's see how much you've learned, my sweet. Let's see how well you can perform under pressure now.'

He pressed a kiss to each of her bare shoulders then she felt his hands at the elastic band of her stockings. He slid them away with her slip and underwear. She heard sounds of him removing his clothes and then seconds later he stretched across her, so his chest brushed her back and shoulders, and he retrieved the small wooden box on the low table beside them.

'I can do rose or almond.' He drew back the box and she lifted her head enough to see it was filled with rose petals and candles and scented oils. 'I was hoping for olive tonight since it's such a special occasion but strangely they haven't supplied any.'

'Perhaps because it makes skin smell like olives?' she ventured faintly. 'Perhaps because, unlike you, most people aren't deviant enough to find that particularly erotic? But it doesn't matter. Massaging each other isn't going to work for me now. Not now that you've put so much stress on me.'

'Oh, yes?' He turned her over so she stared up at him, her eyes wide and accusing, then bent his head and pressed a tiny kiss between her breasts, then more to where her flesh had hardened into little tight beads. 'Too much stress, hmm? That's what you think, is it?'

'Yes.' Unable to stop herself, she arched up and flicked her tongue across his nipples the way they both loved. 'Far too much stress. Forgive me. It'll be better next time, I promise.'

His soft groan increased her courage and her exploration grew bolder as she skimmed one small, outstretched hand lower until his hand curled around her wrist and lifted her away.

'Now that's you, stressing me,' he muttered thickly, and she felt the gratifying rush of his heart against her own as he tipped her back and followed her down. 'Not so fast, my darling. Not tonight. I am nowhere near as in-control of this as I should be. As it is, I think we're going to have to forgo the usual...preliminaries.'

The firm, incredible pressure of his entry made her gasp. She felt stretched, almost painfully at first, but he soothed her and kissed her breasts and gradually her body accommodated itself to him and she felt herself liquefying with delight. His mouth at her breasts sent tremors of fire spiralling across her body, immediately distracting her from her anxiety and when his body, slowly, very slowly, began moving against hers the sensation grew dizzyingly pleasurable.

He caught her to him and held her tight and said her

name over and over, his strokes lengthening and slowing until he filled her senses and everything in the world focused down on to the slow slide of his body within hers and then imploded within her in one fierce contraction of sweet, pure sensation at the same time as he cried out against her.

They lay there for ages, Tessa's head tucked against his shoulder, her body heavy and languid, her breathing slowly, slowly settling, until finally, finally, she could think again. By concentrating as hard as she was capable of doing, she managed to get her eyes open and she turned her head slightly and touched her tongue to the sweat-dampened angle of his jaw. 'I think that must have been my H spot.'

'Which leaves us a lot more alphabet to explore.'

'What I don't understand is how in the world does anybody who can feel that manage to take any interest in life outside of sex?' she demanded brokenly. 'How do people hold down careers? And hobbies? Why on earth do people want to do anything in their lives when they could make love all the time?'

'You have a lot of time to make up.' Nathan's shoulder lifted against her. 'But you'll get used to it. Eventually. As long as you get enough practice.'

'Like maybe in about a hundred years,' she protested.

'Oh, no, that soon will mean lots and lots of practice,' he argued. With a soft groan he tracked his mouth back to hers and Tessa opened her arms to him, her heart swelling with love.

'And lots,' she whispered.

Nathan smiled. 'And then a whole, whole lot more.'

Heartline Books™
Romance at its best!

Your opinion counts!

Last month we published a questionnaire which proved very popular with readers, so we are including it again in our new titles. We want to make sure that we continue to offer you books which are up to the high standard you expect. To do that, we need to know a little more about *you* and your reading likes and dislikes. So please spare a few moments to fill in the questionnaire on the following pages and send it back to us.

Questionnaire

Please tick the boxes to indicate your answers:

1. Did you enjoy reading this Heartline book?

   Title of book: _____

   A lot ☐
   A little ☐
   Not at all ☐

2. What did you particularly like about this book?

   Title of book: _____

   Believable characters ☐
   Easy to read ☐
   Good value for money ☐
   Enjoyable locations ☐
   Interesting story ☐
   Favourite author ☐
   Modern setting ☐

3. If you didn't like this book, can you please tell us why?

   _____

   _____

4. Would you buy more Heartline Books each month if they were available?

   Yes ☐
   No – four is enough ☐

5 What other kinds of books do you enjoy reading?

Puzzle books ☐
Crime/Detective fiction ☐
Non-fiction ☐

Other _____

6 Which magazines and/or newspapers do you read regularly?

a) _____

b) _____

c) _____

d) _____

7 If you received your books by mail order, you will have seen a copy of our newsletter, so can you tell us which parts of the newsletter you find the most interesting?

a) Exclusive celebrity/author interviews?
Interested ☐   Not Interested ☐

b) Competitions, puzzles etc?
Interested ☐   Not Interested ☐

c) Fun starsigns?
Interested ☐   Not Interested ☐

d) Readers' letters?
Interested ☐   Not Interested ☐

What else would you like to see in *your* magazine?

_____

_____

And now a bit about you:

Name _____

Address _____

_____

_____ Postcode _____

Thank you so much for completing this questionnaire.
Now just tear it out and send it in an envelope to:

HEARTLINE BOOKS
FREEPOST LON 16243, Swindon, SN2 8LA

Why not tell all your friends and relatives that they, too, can start a new romance with Heartline Books today by applying for their own, ABSOLUTELY FREE, copy of LOVE IS FOREVER by Natalie Fox. To obtain their free book they can:

- Visit our website www.heartlinebooks.com
- *Or* telephone the Heartline Hotline on 0845 6000504
- *Or* enter their details on the form overleaf, tear it off and send it to:
  Heartline Books
  FREEPOST LON 16243, Swindon, SN2 8LA

And like you they can discover the joys of belonging to Heartline Books Direct

Including:

Four new exciting titles delivered direct to their door every month

A monthly newsletter packed with celebrity interviews, competitions and special offers.

Please send me my free copy of *Love is Forever*:

Name (IN BLOCK CAPITALS)

_____

Address (IN BLOCK CAPITALS)

_____

_____

_____

_____ Postcode _____

If you do not wish to receive selected offers
from other companies, please tick the box ☐

If we do not hear from you within the next ten days, we will be sending you four exciting new romantic novels at a price of £3.99 each, plus £1 p&p. Thereafter, each time you buy our books, we will send you a further pack of four-titles.

Have you missed any of the following sets of books:

The Windrush Affairs *by Maxine Barry*
Soul Whispers *by Julia Wild*
Beguiled *by Kay Gregory*
Red Hot Lover *by Lucy Merritt*

Stay Very Close *by Angela Drake*
Jack of Hearts *by Emma Carter*
Destiny's Echo *by Julie Garrett*
The Truth Game *by Margaret Callaghan*

His Brother's Keeper *by Kathryn Bellamy*
Never Say Goodbye *by Clare Tyler*
Fire Storm *by Patricia Wilson*
Altered Images *by Maxine Barry*

Complete your collection by ringing the Heartline Hotline on 0845 6000504, visiting our website www.heartlinebooks.com or writing to us at Heartline Books, PO Box 400, Swindon SN2 6EJ

Heartline Books...
Romance at its best™